THE MARBLE MOUNTAIN
AND OTHER STORIES

Lisa St Aubin de Terán was born in London in 1953. At the age of sixteen she left James Allen's Girls' School to marry. She and her exiled Venezuelan husband travelled for two years in Italy before returning to his family home in the Andes. After seven years, during which she managed her husband's sugar plantation and avocado farm, she came back to England with her daughter. Lisa St Aubin de Terán is the author of *Keepers of the House*, winner of the Somerset Maugham Award in 1983, *The Slow Train to Milan*, winner of the John Llewellyn Rhys Memorial Prize for 1983, *The Tiger*, *The Bay of Silence*, and *Off the Rails*.

Lisa St Aubin de Terán

THE
MARBLE
MOUNTAIN
AND OTHER STORIES

Pan Books
in association with Jonathan Cape Ltd

First published 1989 by Jonathan Cape Ltd
This edition published 1990 by Pan Books Ltd
Cavaye Place, London SW10 9PG
in association with Jonathan Cape Ltd
9 8 7 6 5 4 3 2 1
© Lisa St Aubin de Terán 1989
ISBN 0 330 31231 6

Printed and bound in Great Britain by
Richard Clay Ltd, Bungay, Suffolk

For Robbie Duff-Scott

Contents

The Marble Mountain

Who could help but be impressed by the marble mountain? Michael Harris stared up at the peaked white giant with its great scars like an opened womb, a constant Caesarean for the goddess of sculpture. Though he had never been to Carrara before, or seen the millennial quarries, this was his world. He knew the different names of the marble, the 'S.1.', the finest marble in the world, white and unveined, unique, used by Michelangelo and thousands of sculptors and masons since. He had come to pay homage, as a sculptor, to the source of his pure white stone.

As he walked up the steep road that wound around the hem-line of the mountain, he felt drawn up into the slopes as though he really did belong there. With his rucksack on his back, packed with his meat rolls and his wine, sketchbook and map, he didn't exactly merge in with the local workmen pruning their vines. But, by his designer jacket and his jeans, his mid-brown hair and the fresh enthusiasm of his face, he could have been Italian. He could have been so many things. It was always the same, no one could clearly tell where he came from. His mother was American, his father, French; he had grown up in England where he passed for one of the lads. But there was always something slightly odd about him, on closer inspection – a Slavic slant to the eyes, a darkness, something that emerged and receded like a narrow tide. So, at a glance, he was always just another stranger, not noteworthy, and not even strange enough to examine more closely and discover the lingering difference. There was something transitory about Michael Harris's looks. Perhaps that was what had guided him into working with stone, a need to carve a permanence of face and limb, a wish to fix everyone's features. Whatever it was, that day, he was just a passing stranger on the hill road out of Carrara on a bright spring morning.

Although it was only ten o'clock, he felt a sudden urge to eat his sandwiches. It was always the same when he carried a picnic: he became like a spendthrift with money in his purse. He told himself that he could sit down in the long grass by the wayside and pretend that he was eating a late breakfast, but the sight of the toiling farmers deterred him. He would wait until he was nearer the quarries. He had been looking forward to taking his first rest somewhere higher up, where the sound of the blasting rock would be near enough for him to see the vast pieces of marble crashing down the precipice of the scar.

Twenty minutes later, he found himself approaching a group of women all looking expectantly down the road at him. He blushed as he walked, wishing that he didn't, but unable to stop it. After he reached them, they continued to stare past him, with such interest that he turned to stare too.

'It's late,' one of them said to him in Italian.

'What is?' he asked, pleased at the correctness of his grammar. He had been studying Italian for years, and he spoke it well, better in fact than French, which was his father's tongue.

'If it hadn't been late, you would have missed it,' the woman told him.

'There isn't another one till ten past two,' another chipped in.

'Yes, ten past two,' they agreed, in chorus.

He was just going to explain that he wasn't waiting for the bus, that he had come to walk and to get a feel of the place, when the bus itself arrived round the nearest bend and braked suddenly beside them. They insisted in letting him on first, jostling him up the step with their enthusiasm. He tried to protest but they would have none of it, he had fallen prey to their concern.

The bus was nearly full; its passengers had been to market and were returning, laden with fruit and fish and vegetables and mops and plastic dustpans and bread, in such a way that there was scarcely anywhere to sit. He moved down the aisle until a small child at the back of the bus was shifted by her mother to make a space for him. At the next stop, three old men got in and blocked the exit with their baskets of tools. Michael sat half-morosely in his seat. He had planned this trip for months, and now, no sooner had it begun than he was losing his grip on it. He could be heading anywhere, and the bus was twisting and turning so that he would have to wait for a village before he got off or he would get lost. He felt for his map in the rucksack on his lap. It was still there, it couldn't really be anywhere else, but he was glad that it was still there.

The road led them round tight bends to a large village. Most of the passengers rose to leave, and Michael rose with them, last in a queue of struggling bundles. The woman who had first spoken to him touched his sleeve.

'Are you going to Bergiola?'

'Yes,' he said, shuffling forwards.

'Then it's the next stop,' she said, pushing him down with such force that he fell into the empty seat beside him. He didn't know where Bergiola was, he'd never heard of it, and now he was left on the half-empty bus with only the women from his stop and a mother and child in the back seat.

The road narrowed from then on, carving a course parallel to the marble mountain itself which came more and more clearly into view. There were chestnut woods on either side of him, with their young pale-green leaves unfurling to cover the bracken and the wild flowers that were growing underneath them. It was steep now, very steep, and every time the bus came to an elbow of black tarmac it sounded its horn. Far in the distance, but brought nearer by their dazzling whiteness, were the quarry faces, while to his left there was a small walled stone cemetery at the end of a path, and to his right some two hundred metres further on there was a small huddled stone village.

'Bergiola,' the driver shouted, and the women smiled, as though confirming his call. Everyone got out now, even the driver, who strolled across a miniature terraced square and disappeared down a narrow alleyway.

There seemed to be no shop or bar or café in the village, so, not knowing where else to go, Michael made his way back down to the cemetery to eat his lunch.

It was a typical Italian *camposànto*: a square of consecrated ground built outside the village by Napoleonic decree. It had the usual network of filled slots in its wall, like a macabre chest of drawers, with black-and-white photographs of the more recently deceased and little urns of plastic flowers. In the far corner, there was a great marble slab, which he sat on, using it as both chair and table, spreading his ham and dry Tuscan bread and his bottle of Chianti wine on the cold stone.

After his meal he would spread his map out on the marble and find out where he was. It was midday, and he was shaken out of his momentary reverie by a thunderous explosion behind him, followed by a long low rumbling of falling stone somewhere in the near distance.

Bergiola was not on the map. He folded the creased sheet of paper away, noticing for the first time that there was something engraved on the slab of stone that he was kneeling on. It was names and dates; a list of names and dates. He began to say them aloud, and his voice gradually dropped to a whisper, hushed by the incantatory quality of the list. There was a strange sameness about it which it took him some time to understand. It read:

> Danzoni Alberto   nato 1916 morto 10-9-1941
> Danzoni Anna   nata 1922 morta 10-9-1941
> Danzoni Antonio   nato 1914 morto 10-9-1941
> Danzoni Beatrice nata 1935 morta 10-9-1941
> Danzoni Carlo   nato 1894 morto 10-9-1941

and so it went on and on, alphabetically through a dynasty of Danzonis, men, women and children of all ages, all dead on the tenth of September 1941.

There were sixty-four names in all, each etched identically in the one slab of marble, and at the end of the list it said simply, 'One unknown woman and one child passing through', and then, 'Another stranger'.

He sat for a long time as though stunned, wondering what to do, as if any action of his could bring back to life any one of them, from Danzoni Enrico, aged seventy-six, to Danzoni Maria

Angela, aged one year. He moved away from the tomb, dusting his crumbs to the earth guiltily.

What had happened in 1941 in a village the size of Bergiola to wipe out so many of its inhabitants? There was a war on all over Europe then, he knew, but what bit of it had found its way up the steep mountain-path to this particular place?

When he finally left the cemetery and the shade of the cypress tree he had been sitting under, he was surprised to find that it was sunny outside. He walked back up to the village itself, pausing to admire the White Lady, the greatest and most plundered and most inexhaustible marble quarry in the world. He had dreamt of this moment, yet, now that it had come, his elation was poisoned by the litany of names. He heard a tuneless whistling coming up the hill towards him and turned to discover its source. An old man with a fine peasant's face, weathered like a block of stone and dressed in an incongruously smart tweed suit, was approaching. He, too, paused by the view of the marble mountain, making an almost imperceptible obeisance to her, before shouting, 'Buongiorno', to Michael.

'Buongiorno,' he replied, but before he could phrase any of the questions that were forming in his mind, the man was gone, wheezing slightly and whistling the same out-of-tune and unrecognizable snatch of song.

The village itself had an air both of prosperity and desolation, with the houses either completely abandoned or exceptionally well-maintained. Outside the village, but bordering on it, there stood a large, once formal garden run to seed. The avenues of low box-hedges had grown to unruly bushes, and, where the light permitted, into small trees. There were statues and a fountain strangled by ivy and moss and weeds. There were ornamental trees growing into each other, all fighting for the available space, while, here and there beneath them, clumps of lilies, irises and tangled roses continued to flourish, defiantly ignoring their years of neglect. A few of the lilies were even in flower, and from the crumbling outer wall of the garden, Michael could smell their sweetness triumphing over the dank pervading odour of leaf-mould. Almost out of sight, at the far end of this garden, trapped in a thicket of climbing plants, there was a *càsa nobile* – a country house – the sort of house that bore ancestral coats of arms over its door and windows: a once stuccoed, Palladian villa. It too bore every sign of abandon.

The stillness of this house and its grounds suited Michael's mood, and he sat on the damp stone wall for a long time trying to imagine who had lived there and why such a fine house should be reduced to such a sorry state. At first, he thought the list of names could have lived there; and yet there were too many of them. It was, indeed, a large house, from what he could make out, but not large enough, he felt. There were so many Danzonis that it seemed to be all one family, but there had been other names as well, perhaps the desolation of this house was in some way the key to that mass grave.

He was so deep in thought, that he didn't even hear the old man approaching him this time, and his loud 'Buona sera' startled him.

'Buona sera,' he replied, and then added hastily, lest the old man should leave again, 'it's strange, all this, it looks so abandoned.'

'There are stranger things than that here,' the old man shouted, and then paused, offering his hand. 'I am Gabriele,' he said, again in a voice so loud, that it was clear that he must be deaf.

Michael introduced himself, raising his voice several decibels to do so, and Gabriele nodded, pleased.

'Well done,' he said, 'well done, you speak loudly. We are all deaf here, in Bergiola, all us men, it's from working in the quarries, after a while the dynamite dulls every other sound.' He shrugged, as though his hearing had never been of much importance to him.

'So you were a quarryman,' Michael said.

'Huh,' Gabriele smiled. 'A quarryman! Why, I know every inch of the quarries here about, and on the other side. In fact,' he announced proudly, 'there are not many quarries that I don't know. I have been to France, and Germany and all over Italy – where there is stone to be blasted, that's where I've been.'

A short silence settled between them, broken at last by, 'Why did you go abroad when the best quarries are here on your doorstep?'

'No problem,' Gabriele said, 'I'll tell you, I went to eat, and to support my family. We in Bergiola have no other trade, we were born to quarry, we live by it, when there is no work here, we have to migrate, like birds, to follow the jobs, to find the food.'

It was cold sitting on the wall, the damp from the garden had permeated the air. Michael shivered a little, and shifted his position on the damp stone.

'Would you like a coffee,' Gabriele asked, dipping his hand into his pocket as though he were about to pull out a cup of it then and there.

'Yes please.'

'Come on then, we'll go to my house. I saw you looking at the white mountain earlier, it's a fine sight.'

Michael stood up, and followed him back through the narrow uneven street to the village square and, from there, past a bronze water-pump cast in the form of a cat chasing a rat. What had seemed to him to be one street forming the top side of the square turned out to be one enormous farmhouse into which they went. He followed the old man down a rambling corridor past room after room stretching out like bones on a fish-spine. Each room seemed to have a very scant, nominal use. So one room was littered only with paper sacks, and one with trays of potatoes; another had some disused baskets while yet another had a pair of crumpled shirts to iron and an old blanket spread over a pine table as a makeshift ironing board. At the end of this corridor was a kitchen, with a small cast-iron stove upon which a pot of clear broth was bubbling. In the corner there was a large, very modern gas-cooker with an eye-level grill and a number of fancy extras all sealed still from the factory, and wrapped in a huge sheet of thick polythene. The room, like the village, showed a great mixture of expensive new additions and worn decaying ones.

Gabriele approached the fire and kicked its hot cast-iron pot-belly, producing a shower of small sparks from its glowing seams.

'The mountain,' he said, half to the stove and half to his guest, 'is like a beautiful woman, like a Madonna, and we, we are like insects scratching at her face. She is always there, always bountiful. Of course, if you are careless, she will break you . . . but what beautiful woman will not avenge a betrayal?'

He motioned to Michael to sit down, which he did, on a woven plastic chair. Gabriele now moved to an old marble sink and began to fiddle with a tiny coffee-machine. He caught Michael's glance as it returned from the wrapped cooker.

'My daughter wanted me to buy it,' he explained, 'so I did, but what use is a thing like this to an old man? At least the neighbours can say, "Gabriele has a really fine cooker", and my daughter can feel proud of her father. These are the times we have come to. It is a luxury; but it is more of a luxury to have the time to consider it one.'

Having spent what he felt to be a decent length of time toying with the coffee-apparatus, he drew up a litre of red wine from behind a small curtain and offered it instead, pouring two tumblerfuls with an alacrity that he seemed to have hitherto lacked in his kitchen.

'I started working when I was twelve, always quarrying, always here. We set off at dawn, a whole troop of us from the village, and we worked harder than a boy like you could know. My father and my grandfather and his grandfather had all worked in the lap of the White Lady. We never imagined it could end. Then Mussolini came, and the Three Powers silenced her groan. What does it mean to be a Power? I never understood what made them that – England, France, and America – no, I never knew, but they had the power to scatter this village. They didn't approve of Mussolini, so they boycotted certain things, and Carrara marble was one of them. They were the buyers, those Three Powers, and they stopped importing so we had to stop exporting and gradually the piles of hewn rock grew so big that we had to stop quarrying. I went to France, and then to Germany; the others from the village went away too. Some of them went to America and never came back, but mostly we worked for our families, and we all returned.

'It would have been better if we'd left the village altogether and taken our families with us and never come back. But it was our village, our world, and we didn't know what was going to happen. Who could imagine such a pitiless thing? . . . Only a sick man.'

Michael sipped his wine, it had a slight sourness to it, as though home-made. Gabriele gulped his, swilling it back in one go and then refilling his glass with gusto. 'Good, eh?' he said, referring to the wine.

His hands were very finely veined, Michael noticed now, veined and flecked like some beautiful, third or fourth quality marble, not of the kind that was used for statues, but of the kind that was used for steps and facings. Each line was a thin scar and each scar joined another making a network of old injuries along the old man's fists and fingers.

'I was in Frankfurt when the War broke out, I had searched for work there doing what I knew, but there wasn't any. I thought unemployment was Italian, just something that had happened to us. Being out of work is like snow, you see it fall on your village and you think that elsewhere it will be clear, so you set off for the next village and, of course, the snow is there too. So it was with the work, there was none here, there was none there.

'I got a job working as a cook. Well, unskilled, you can't cook in Italy, but there, what do they eat? Potatoes and cabbage, and pork and potatoes, even Gabriele could manage that. I cooked in a soldiers' mess. Big tubs of cabbage, vats of sausage. I carried the food through to the serving tables. One day, I was carrying a tray of sausages through, and I heard the shouting and the cheering and I listened through the swing door. Krieg, that's what they call it. I turned right round with my tray of sausages and I went right back through the kitchen. "Where are you going?" the chef shouted. "Just a minute," I said, "Moment," and out through the back door and on and on. When I reached the gate I left the sausages, inside, and I kept going till I got back to Bergiola. I couldn't send my wages back with a war on, could I?'

He paused to rummage in the many inner pockets of his tweed jacket and then found what he wanted in a misshapen packet of black cigarettes which he put on the oilcloth table-cover, offering to share them.

'I wasn't back long, just long enough to make another child,

another mouth to feed, and then I went into the hills to join
the Partisans. And I still fed my family, from the hills, we used
to take it in turns to creep back to the village with provisions.

'The Partisans were strong here, they had been strong against
Mussolini when he was on his own, and they were strong still
when the Germans came. Everyone was joining, but they made
so many groups that the men didn't know where to join.
Sometimes there would be three or four boys out in the hills
alone, like bandits. They often did more harm than good.

'The Germans didn't hate us Italians, they despised us, and
maybe that is worse. They used to come to Bergiola to admire
the White Lady, because they loved Art. Every statue from
here to Calabria was wrapped in straw and crated and sent by
rail back to Germany, so they liked to come with their smart
cars that could scarcely get up the hill, and stare at the marble
mountain.

'Carrara itself had a pact with the Germans, I don't know
how or why, but no reprisals ever fell on Carrara. Even things
that happened there were avenged on the surrounding villages,
so all the little hamlets copped it, one after another. For every
German soldier who was killed here, three Italians had to die.
They chose them at random from the villages, just "you, you
and you" and then shot them in the square. For an officer it
was six. They thought they were worth three of us, six of us,
no wonder they treated us like scum.

'It looked as though Bergiola was lucky, saved somehow by
the mountain's stare, because they hardly ever came this far.
The road was worse then, much worse, and their regulation
cars weren't made for such gradients.'

Old Gabriele lit a cigarette, steadying his right hand with his
left to do so, propping one batch of scars up with the other.
Michael remained very still, not wanting to interrupt the old
man's flow. He felt both a dread gathering in the pit of his
stomach with the sour wine, and a curiosity to know the worst
and be done with it.

'Somewhere on the low road that cuts from Carrara to the
track that curves around the foot of the mountain, a German
soldier was shot. One German soldier on a motorbike. He came
off somewhere near the large loop, and they found him the

next day in the river. Nobody knew who shot him. It wasn't us, and everybody else said it wasn't them. I was in the hills that day with my group, up behind the small quarry where there are caves to hide in and a lot of chestnut trees for camouflage.

'It was four o'clock when the Germans arrived, not one carful, but five in the square. Four o'clock, so the women were fetching water from the pump, and children were playing and the old men were out on the bench gossiping and wheezing. They were the first to be counted, the ones in the square and in the street. They were taken down to the old school house. A teacher and some children were already in there, so they were counted too. Then they began to go from door to door, taking whoever answered and whoever was hidden behind them. Soon there were more than thirty in the one room of the schoolhouse. Nobody knew what they were being taken for, not at first.

'You remember the big house where we met; the garden?'

Michael nodded.

'There was a captain in the Italian Army who'd been wounded and invalided out. He was a lawyer before and that's what he did again. He used to go down to Carrara every day and come back in the evening to his wife and child. They had just the one child, a little boy. They were like children themselves, all full of love. We didn't used to care for them in the village, I suppose because they had no time for us, so we had none for them. They were too engrossed with themselves, what time could they have had over? They weren't local. He'd bought the house, for her, after it was confiscated.

'While her husband was away at work, she used to take her little boy for walks in their garden, and sometimes, but not often, she would take him walking outside the village, gathering wild flowers and things. The few times she'd come through the village, she'd walked by as though it wasn't there. We were invisible to her, the little boy could see us all right, but he was all for copying his mother.

'Even love isn't blind to five German cars parked in a tiny square, though, so when she walked by with her little bunch of daisies that day, she said, "Buona sera," and both of them were counted. Two words, two heads. That was when the others began to panic. If the Captain's wife was being dragged down to the schoolhouse, then heaven help the rest. So, the next house they came to, no one would answer the door. The soldiers kicked it in. They found three women in the kitchen and they shot them then and there. Those who saw it say that that was when the screaming began, because now everybody knew what the Germans were counting for, and they wanted sixty-three people. Most of us men were gone, to soldier for Mussolini or for the Partisans or still abroad. Only the sick and wounded were there, and the very young and old, the rest were women.

'Then the soldiers divided, so they say, half to the old schoolhouse, and half round the village, banging on doors and shooting through windows and dragging people out into the street by their hair. Grandmothers and babies and nursing mothers were all just numbers that day and never enough numbers to make up the quota.

'From where I was, in the hills, I couldn't hear the shooting, I was already deaf from dynamiting, and I couldn't hear the shouting, though some of the boys with me said they could. What I heard was the high-pitched shrieking, which must have been the women and the children. I heard that from the first great scream when they set the school alight. I didn't hear the shooting as they picked out the ones who managed to escape the fire and run into the playground half-alight. I didn't hear them gun them down till not a living thing was left inside. All I heard was the shrillness and the terror that came right up to where we were though it was some miles away. We could see the smoke, a huge black cloud of greasy smoke, and as we ran and fell down to our houses, we smelt its clinging, cloying smell and we were sick.

'When they had reached their number, sixty-three, they turned and left, and the handful of people who had survived came out to count their dead. Everyone lost somebody, and some of us lost everyone. By the time we men arrived, the blood was running in the streets, Danzoni blood.

'What can you think of something like that, what can you say? It makes your mind break. It makes you cling to the old things you know, like friends, like the friends who are dead.

We have so much money now in the village; all the rooms and riches of the ones who died.

'You know, before the Germans left that day, the Captain came home early from work. He went to greet his wife, and the servant told him what had happened. He couldn't believe it. He was stunned, wandering round the house shouting, and then he went into the square. His servant tried to stop him, but he shook her off. He went right up to the German commanding officer and demanded to know where his wife and son were, but he could already see signs of the massacre at his feet, the square was full of bodies. He still didn't believe it, so he went down to the schoolhouse which was down but burning. He poked around the charred remains of the corpses in the playground, until he found his wife, by the rings on her fingers, and he went back to the commanding officer, and he shouted at him, "Shoot me, too."

'The German refused. They wanted sixty-three, and they had sixty-three. The job was done.

'Then the Captain said, "You have destroyed all that matters to me in life, please kill me, too."

'So the German took out his pistol and shot him through the head. Sixty-four.

'We put the Captain and his wife together. We made just one grave for all of them, because they had all died together. Nobody ever cared much from down below. No one came from Carrara. We dug our own pit, and we put our family in it, and the Captain's, and a poor woman who had come to the village that day, no one knew why, with her child in her arms – half-crazed she was, they say – and another stranger, a man who had lost his way.'

Old Gabriele's voice trembled a little as he spoke the last words of his shouted monologue. He stared at a small patch of ash under his stove, and then shuddered.

'The last bus will be turning shortly . . . you'd better be on your way.'

Michael rose, obediently and silently, to leave. He was called back before he got halfway to the door.

'I've thought about it these forty years, and there isn't any sense in it. Lately, though, I just try to get through the hours of the day. Soon all I'll be able to hear will be the thunder of the White Lady, and then, one day, I'll go where I belong, with my family. That's where a man does belong, you know, with his family.'

Outside the window, below in the square, the straining of a bus engine could be heard.

'I'll see you out,' the old man said, sidling ahead of Michael and back down the now dark corridor to the front door.

'Arrivederci . . .' He paused, searching for a name, but finding none he gave his own, holding out his scar-veined hand to shake, 'I am Gabriele, Danzoni Gabriele.'

I Never Eat Crabmeat Now

Looking back, I don't know what is worse to live with; I suppose I just try and forget what I can. There are some things that never go away though, like the smell worming its way back into everything and clinging to the inside of my brain; and then the Daily still missing Fred and asking after him. Then pushchairs, and fish shops just make me feel sick. Last week I saw a budgerigar in a cage picking at a cuttle-fish bone, and that triggered everything off again; now I can't sleep for thinking about Amadeo. What was it? I feel I'll never really sleep well again until I know, but I realize that I might not sleep at all if I really knew the truth.

Why did you go to Diélette, a place you'd never even heard of before, a place nobody seems to have heard of? What was the allure of that desolate stretch of Normandy with nothing but sand and stone and discontent wedged into its disproportionate harbour? 'Why go anywhere?' you had said, and shrugged, and I knew that your restlessness was impenetrable then, at least by me. I contemplated trying to hold you back, detain you by some devious means, but I believed your indifference to be incurable. Wherever you went you would look out to sea, scanning the horizon for someone or something you missed. You lived in a state of orchestrated lack; when there was no sea you would invent it. It was just another layer of your dream, like me, to be peeled away and discarded at will; and then drawn back in from time to time to wrap around you. You were locked in fantasy, turning the weeds of our back garden into waves. Our house was like a mad-house again. You read my thoughts and said: 'The only incurable thing about me is my need for movement.'

I wasn't impressed, since you refused to take me, or rather let me go in any capacity. I tried to understand this need of yours for solitude, but when I saw that you intended to travel with your customary circus, I was so annoyed that I didn't even haggle over the terms of my defeat.

You moved with a troupe of girls ranging from late adolescence through the various stages of precocious delinquency and charm, compromising only with the androgynous Amadeo in his pram with his angelic curls and frills. It struck a genuine chord of consolation, the only one, to be released from Amadeo's distressing eating habits for a month. Apart from that, he was the only one who ever really accepted me. He managed with his smile to make me an honorary girl like him. Unlike the others – our twins, eight years old and congenitally impossible. I used to worry that they might be autistic, but they were just savages. Then there was their nanny, the luscious but otherwise singularly useless Candy, and her 'little sister' Rachel. I don't know what possessed you to take Rachel. Ever since she had installed herself, uninvited, in the spare bedroom the year before she had done nothing but vent her nymphomania on the neighbourhood and breed resentment.

You took them all with you, though, that potentially lethal human zoo, as though in your inner loneliness you found security in clutter. You even drugged the cat and put it in the picnic basket, and smuggled Fred the tortoise across the Channel in a hollow compartment of the pram. And Fred was my tortoise, too – but then Amadeo was my son.

I went as far as Waterloo and saw you off. The station was insufferable, inundated with people and luggage, and most of the luggage seemed to be yours. You billeted your party around the cafeteria and then sat down to your toast. It was dry and hard and you became obsessed by it. Whatever I said, you came back to that toast. 'I actually can't chew it. What is it made of? What is one supposed to do with it?' Amadeo, temporarily released, had spread raspberry jam on his, and was intent on wiping it off across the table-tops and people's knees. You were too involved, however, in the nature of the bread to notice, and the girls paid no attention. Only the newly-spread fellowbreakfasters retreated one by one, protesting and ignored by you.

Nobody could staunch your urge to travel, but in the more practical aspects of your life, even you had to give way occasionally. Getting the three-foot-six-inch pram through the three-foot door of the train to Portsmouth was one such example. Amadeo got a foretaste of the seasickness to come, rammed and battered against the ungiving hinges of the door, while you charged at the inadequate space time and again. I don't know if it was fascination or despair that stopped me from intervening. If the guard hadn't come and taken you through the double doors of his wagon, I suppose I would have done something, if only for poor Fred.

After you'd left, I began to hate Diélette. It just seemed wrong from the start: it wasn't on the maps, people didn't go there. You said you were going for just that, to hide away in a fishing village in a land of warm bread. How do you hide with four extravagant females in your wake, and an overgrown baby? And that stale station toast only came up during your departure; we always ate fresh bread from the *pâtisserie* at South End Green. It wasn't what I felt that seemed to matter then or now, so much as what happened to you and the others.

I've pieced together what I can, from you, from the twins and from my own trip out after your phone call. So I know that you sailed to Cherbourg and arrived somehow and disembarked out of the bowels of an impersonal ferry and then ferried your troupe by taxi to the Hôtel de France there. You stayed for one night only, anxious to move on to Diélette, that unknown place of your perverse dream. Amadeo always had to sleep alone: the slightest intrusion would wake him, and once his usual almost narcoleptic sleep had been disturbed, he would cry and moan all night. In the absence of a cot, Rachel made him a mattress of pillows inside a capacious wardrobe, and then locked him in. When the maid unlocked the door on an apparently empty room and was met by a piercing cry from the coffin-like wardrobe in question, she dropped her breakfast-tray and ran.

* * *

'What kind of mother would do such a thing?' the taxi driver who was taking me to Diélette asked after he had regaled me with the details of this apparently iniquitous neglect. I didn't attempt to explain that Amadeo liked contained spaces and the dark. The driver remembered you clearly and needed no prompting to unravel a list of further aberrations. He referred to you as 'the Lady with the strange eyes', and he told me, in his clear coastal French, how he had enjoyed sitting beside you for the half-hour of the ride. He explained that he had been feeling nervous the day he drove you, and the thought of going to Diélette had filled him with dread, but that your presence had somehow calmed him down. I remember I warmed to the man for understanding these things. He seemed nervous, though, again with me.

'The baby carriage scratched all the paint off my car,' he said. 'I didn't want to charge her for it, but . . . even if she'd been the blessed Virgin herself – a man has to live.'

He shrugged, and we drove on in silence for some minutes, well away now from the prim shuttered rows of houses and the outlying estates of modern flats. That was when I started to feel sick. On either side of the road, mixed hedges straggled into small, well tended fields interrupted by the occasional *hameau* of grey stone houses. It was unnaturally hot, and every time I paused to think about it, it seemed to be getting hotter.

As we passed through Virandeville the taxi swerved to avoid a group of conscripts who looked as though their feet had melted into the tarmac. The driver whistled angrily through his teeth. 'Some people like trouble.'

I nodded.

'They look for it,' he said.

Again, I agreed politely.

'That lady of yours, she is like that,' he smiled with a mixture of horror and admiration.

We drove on, faster now, as though to prove that he too could be reckless when he chose.

'And why go to Diélette?'

I found myself repeating your own words. 'Why go anywhere?'

'Yes, yes . . . but Diélette, ever since they put the nuclear plant there five years ago, it is not the same place, not what it seems; there's something bad there now, you can feel it in the air. It isn't safe, especially not for her — not for those girls either.'

He paused, and I sat back uneasily.

'They're riff-raff, not even French,' he said, jerking left to bypass Les Pieux, 'they're Arabs.' He paused again.

'If it weren't for the crabs, God knows what there would be found floating in the sea.'

'Crabs?' I repeated, holding back a wave of nausea as the taxi charged yet another hill in third gear.

'That's what they used to fish for.'

'Used to?'

'There's hardly anyone left now, of the old lot, and those that are are fishing for trouble.'

The driver was impressed into momentary silence, then the spectre of the sea came into view from over a hill, and he shuddered, and his voice seemed to break loose again, insinuating its way into my innermost thoughts like the frothing rope of spume dragging at the sand.

Outside Cherbourg, when we passed our first ribbon of grey stone cottages — the *boulangerie*, bar and that straggling row of identical dwellings — it struck me that they were spaced almost as though they were afraid to huddle together, like defeated soldiers limping back to some familiar ground. At first that air of semi-regimented despair had seemed quaint, but as we passed one hamlet after another, each as grey and as unforgiving as the last, I grew tired of them. Until that half-hour ride to Diélette, I didn't know I could grow tired of a colour so quickly, but that greyness showed me: the walls were grey, and the road, and the sides of rocks that occasionally overhung the road, and the gulls and houses, and the sky, for all its heat, still shimmered grey, and even the skin of the peasants peering out from behind grubby curtains was grey. Only the greens, the oaks and sycamores and the turning green of the ripening corn contrasted with the dour twilight shades. By Les Pieux, though, the drone of my driver's voice had so effectively blended with the forced roar of his engine and my own fears as to make me believe that the green itself was a tremendous growth of mould.

When the sea came into view I felt a kind of dizziness grip the back of my head. It was hard to breathe in the heat. The tide was low and I felt, looking at the sweep of dunes and rock that joined the sea to dry land, that it was pulling and grasping at all it could, at me on the hill, at the taxi, at the haze of sand, sucking it out into its mysterious depths and giving nothing back. The driver matched my mood with one of sombre reserve: where before he had talked out of a wish to communicate, he spoke now out of a reluctant need to annihilate silence. This time round, though, I refused to listen. I had the sea to torment me now, so I blocked out his ramblings about the evils of the nuclear plant and the alleged bandits that ran it. Instead, I dreamt that I had buried my head somewhere in those coves of bleached sand, and the sea was dragging out my entrails.

It was only meant to be four more miles to Diélette, and the taxi was doing a steady fifty, and yet that last lap from the crest of the hill to you was the slowest. I could drown the monologue beside me, but I could not ignore the heat or the strange atmosphere. It was like stepping off an aeroplane into the tropics. My ankles were beginning to swell, and they got worse as we crawled towards our destination. The air-conditioning appeared to have broken down. I opened the window on my side, but the driver shook his sweating face sadly.

'That'll only make it worse.'

By the time we entered the village itself, I realized that your description of the house was a useless guide to finding it. I was there because of your strange call; you had spent most of the time saying my name, and then repeating over and over again, 'Are you there?' The line was crackling, and somewhere, an irate operator was cutting in. I heard you say, 'Come,' and something about Amadeo and his pram; and then you had said, as an afterthought, I suppose, 'The house is grey.'

The taxi driver tried to leave me at the crossroads, but I

refused to get out there. I knew he must know where to go to find you in that exposed warren. We climbed the hill to Flamanville and away from the stark sign pointing to the nuclear plant and the beach. For once, he was driving slowly. The last lap of the route had smelt like a fishing village with its sour barnacled odour of stale shellfish and damp nets. I had noticed little piles of dead crabs and their remains outside one or two of the houses. We stalled outside a row of three tall cottages standing on their own. The driver seemed unwilling either to stop or get out of the car. He pointed to the middle door and asked for two hundred francs. I opened my door and remained half-in and half-out. I paid him and straightened my crumpled clothes.

'*Quel molosse!*' he whispered, letting the banknotes fall to the taxi floor, then he drove off up the hill with the car door swinging free. I looked in the direction of his last horrified stare, and saw an enormous slavering hound straining at a rusty chain in the next doorway. I flattened myself instinctively against the wall and watched while an elderly man, wearing the traditional *bleu*, stumbled out after the dog. It appeared to be a hybrid race somewhere between an alsatian and a bear, a brown shaggy matted beast with huge teeth and yellow eyes. The man dragged it back in with great difficulty, and I nodded to him, but he was so drunk I couldn't tell whether he could see me or not. He gave the impression of not having managed to focus on anyone for years.

There were flies everywhere. Outside your door there was a heap of long-dead crabs looking more deliberately gathered or discarded than elsewhere. As I knocked on the door, a wizened face appeared at the window of your other neighbour. This time, when I nodded, I was met by a chilled stare before the ancient face disappeared, letting the cobbled net curtain slip back into place. Although most of your windows were broken, your door was locked; and the house seemed deserted. I thanked God that I wasn't travelling with the kind of luggage you always trailed behind you, picked up my holdall and made my way back down to the village and the beach – where else would you be at lunch-time in this heat? It was a relief to be away from the taxi, there had been something sinister about his manner. I went into a little bar and drank a Cognac. The locals were engrossed in a game of cards, so they scarcely looked when I went in, and although the barmaid was sour to me, she had a sour face and lines around her mouth that came from more than just ignoring me that day. I asked about you, and she shrugged; when I asked again, she smiled knowingly. I was not deterred though, I had travelled across the Channel often enough to know the low opinion that all Frenchmen have of my French. Then I went out and down the coast road for a hundred yards or so. There was the lighthouse standing out on its stone rampart, the abandoned harbour, and the massive nuclear plant on one side, barely visible beyond a beach. And then on the other side there was a stretch of sand and rocks curving round for mile upon mile lined by low cliffs and fields. It was a magnificent view, and I felt that you would be out that way. After twenty minutes of trekking over the hot sand, it was a mystery to me how you could have gone further with the pram and the circus and the picnic that you would inevitably have brought. But by then I was too hot to bother, and I sat down to rest. I think I sat and stared at the bare cuttle-fish bones and the circling gulls and at the sea itself, and then I buried my face in my bag and fell asleep.

I woke up, hours later, feeling dizzy from the sun. I scanned the littered shore for you, but the beach was deserted. That was when I started feeling really angry. I resented your indifference, and your alternate clinging and rejection. Disappearing then into the fifth dimension just seemed to me to be another example of your perversity. I vented my wrath on the stray bladderwracks, bursting the drying sacks of brine. Where I had thought to find you lying waiting, there were only the torn pincers of crabs, and little piles of dismembered limbs quilted in flies' wings. I walked back past the bar and on across the sands in the opposite direction, and I was unconsciously gathering bits of crab and consciously thinking bad things about you when I saw the pram.

It was standing on its own, as lifeless in its way as the lighthouse, but I didn't see that at first. It had what appeared

to be a new dark sunshade, and between me and it, the twins
were digging in the sand. As I approached them, they looked
up once, but made no sign of recognition. They were burnt the
colour of Baltic pine, and their hair looked almost irrevocably
tangled; they seemed so intent on shovelling their sand that I
thought they were purposely ignoring me. Even when I stood
right beside them, they kept shovelling, manically, heaping up
the slipping sand into a long mound.

'Aren't you going to say hello?' I asked.

'We're burying crabs.'

'Where's mummy?'

'She's back at the house, she doesn't come out any more.'

There was a strange smell of old crab meat, of beach debris,
of shells and fish and rotting flesh in the sun, and then an
undertow of something else. It mixed in with the heat and made
me feel physically sick. Halfway to the pram, the twins stopped
again, shaking out their frilly swimming things and then squar-
ing themselves to dig once more. They marked out a rectangle
some three feet by one.

'Still burying crabs?'

'Yup.'

'Why?'

'They've eaten Rachel,' one of them told me, then the other
one interrupted, 'Well, she fell in the sea, actually.'

'. . . and then they ate her!'

They had stopped digging now, and were poised to fight, with
their eight-year-old fists trembling to be right.

'When did Rachel fall in the sea?' I asked patiently. They
both paused and a sudden wave of boredom registered on their
identical faces.

'Oh, ages ago.'

It was their boredom that made me fear for Amadeo,
since they too, like you, were irritated by certain aspects of
reality.

I couldn't get to the pram without my handkerchief as a gag. I
cursed the place that had nothing but bad feelings and dead
crabs, and I was angry for once with the twins for using the
pram as a sea hearse. When I looked in, I was too shocked to

even be sick. I pushed it blindly through the haze of hovering flies, struggling to force its wheels through the dry sand. The twins were calling now but their voices were as unintelligible as the gulls to me. Then one of them was tugging at my shirt.

'Don't go that way, daddy, that's the Centrale, it's bad, that's where the smell comes from.'

I tried to push on, but they blocked the way of the pram, staring down sadly at Amadeo's prostrate body. His hair was bleached almost white, and his face was parched and peeling, his lips cracked and caked with dry blood where he had been mouthing, and the frills of his lace shirt looked more like layers of a soiled dressing. He lay completely dull and listless, incarcerated by the abominable smell.

'How long has he been in there?'

'Oh, ages.'

'Jesus!'

They seemed annoyed suddenly as though by my stupidity.

'He can't hold up his head. He can't do that since we went to the Centrale. He's got the sickness, and so has mummy. Mummy's hiding at the house. She says she has to stay in the dark, and Amadeo has to stay in the sun.'

'Why?'

'Because of the smell, of course. But you mustn't take him near the Centrale, or she'll be furious.'

Amadeo whimpered when I touched him, so I didn't dare lift him out. Instead, I pushed the pram back up the slope. The villagers were there, staring. I noticed that the ones who had tolerated me at the bar were now out on the street, frowning and muttering too. Someone spat as the twins passed, and the gobbet fell a few inches away from their sandalled feet.

'Why do they hate us like this?'

The twins didn't seem to mind.

'I suppose because of the smell; they hate most things.'

'Like what?'

'Like the Centrale, and Rachel, and the others.'

Even with Rachel in the sea, only four were accounted for, that left one more of your circus to account for.

'Where is Candy?' I asked, hopefully, I don't know why.

'She's gone.'

'Where?'

'Just gone.'

I didn't ask any more questions after that, I didn't want to be told any more answers. The twins wanted things, they wanted gobstoppers from the slot machine outside the shop, and they wanted new spades to bury more crabs and they wanted horsemeat for the cat; but I didn't dare go into that shop, it was all I could do to walk past the villagers, shoving that foul stench up the hill and watching them exchange their looks as we passed. The twins walked ahead of me, apparently unconcerned by the fuss. As we neared the crossroads I felt myself leaning more and more heavily on the pram as my knees weakened from the excessive heat and the smother of Amadeo. A fat slow-eyed cadet was leaning against a wall, he looked about sixteen and very sweaty. As the twins passed him, he lunged forward, trying to touch the nearest on her flat sunburnt chest. As he reached out, he leered at me with an unpleasant complicity. I didn't see what happened next, but the soldier pulled his hand back bleeding from a deep gash.

'Putains,' he said and turned back to the wall, clutching his wound.

The twins were proud of themselves, and they showed me the sharpened cuttle-fish bones they were holding in their hands.

'They're not going to touch us.'

'Not after what they did to Rachel.'

'What did they do to Rachel?' I asked, despite myself, breaking my earlier vow of silence.

'Well they're not going to do it to us,' they said firmly and then continued up the hill, swinging their worn spades.

I never liked Rachel, you know, and I didn't want to know what they had done, had they pushed her into the sea or had she fallen, or had she jumped because of something else they did to her, or were the twins lying, they did after all, lie a lot.

I didn't care somehow, not for Rachel or the others really. I
had to care about Amadeo, and keeping the flies off him, and
getting him back, and somehow making the twins be eight
again, and most of all I had to find you.

When we reached the house the drunkard was sitting out by
the road fondling his dog.

'That's Pierre,' one of the twins whispered, then: 'Hello,
Pierre.'

He stared at her, looking somewhere halfway between
her and her double, looking confused, probably seeing four
girls instead of two. He turned his head away without reply-
ing.

'He never talks,' they explained.

The door was still locked when I tried it, but the twins had
gone on past the house, beckoning me round after them. I
pushed on up a dirt track, feeling that at any moment the pram
would run back over me. Once in the back garden, there was a
tiny flight of stairs to negotiate, then a footbridge, and then a
door.

'What about 'Deo?'

'Oh we always leave him here, you can't get it down the
steps, it'd tip.'

There was a view out over roof-tops and the bay, curving slowly
round to the tip of Normandy. I tried to lift poor
'Deo out again then, but he was stuck to the mattress, and
the smell when I moved it was more than I could bear, and I
gagged.

'You do go on about it,' one of the twins moaned. 'We've
been living with it for weeks.'

There were, it seemed incongruously, a briar rose and a
sweetpea growing out of the nettles that lined the steps.

Why were you hiding in the closet? Who were you hiding
from? You'd always had such an array of camp followers,
why had they suddenly gone? You just wept, you wouldn't
tell me anything, and now – you still won't tell me. Amadeo
was my son, I want to know. I could have sworn I felt him
whimper in the pram, but now I know that it was just the

flies. When I came to bury him, he was rigid and had been for God knows how long. Was that all you called me for, to bury the baby? What would you have done if I hadn't come? And I wonder, what strange thing has settled over that village that lets a dead child wander up and down stinking the place out and no one intervene? Were they all child molesters, as the twins imply? Or was there radiation sickness, as you seem to think? I wish I knew what you did think, and sometimes, if you think at all. Life is all toast to you, how do they make it? why do we eat it? what is it there for?

It's just you and me now, and the *pâtisserie* at South End Green, and the croissants on Sundays. At night sometimes I just lie awake and wonder, who did what to the baby?

I would have taken him to the police, but there was no one to take him to. And then there was something about your crying that frightened me. What would you say to the police? And what about Rachel? And could the twins be trusted not to say something outrageous, not to lie. . . ? By the next morning, I felt that smell was in my hair, behind my eyes, everywhere. I suppose that was why I buried him. It seemed the least I could do really. I put him in the sand, one night's digging deep. I expect he's still there.

When I go down to Kent now to visit the twins at school, I have to force myself not to ask them about 'Deo, and I find myself looking at them in a funny way, wondering if they could have done such a thing. If it wasn't them, was it you? Who did it? And why in Diélette? The ferry back was a nightmare: I got so seasick I thought I'd turn inside out over the rail, thinking about Amadeo in the sand, and Fred, poor Fred rotted down to a puddle under his shell inside the pram. By the time I got to him I'd had enough, I couldn't even bring myself to tip him out, so he's still rotting there, rusting into the garden with its beautiful view – there didn't seem any point in lugging the pram back empty.

So some nights I can't sleep, and some nights you can't either. Meanwhile, we've got your wretched toast to discuss; and now the wonder is wearing off, finally, after all these years,

I don't know what to do with you; but I've had a vasectomy —
just in case; and I never touch crabmeat now, of any kind, not
even in a sandwich. And every summer, when the swelter sets
in, I get an urge to go back to Diélette.

Diamond Jim

They call it Tarlojee, that grey stretch of land that fans out from the Essequibo and it's got a strange history buried under every rock and tree. It's a stony place, and where the fields have been cleared, and the sugar grows and flowers with its grey fluff, the piles of stones make little hills like shrines in places. No wonder, then, that people forget the past when there's so much of it and all heaped up like that. So, who came and when, and whether they were Dutch or Scots or Portuguese, and whether they were good or bad, stayed or died, nobody really cares or knows on Tarlojee.

The sun is too hot there to go filling your head with tales. It's enough to remember where the shifting sands lie along the river, and where the snakes are worst, and which of the many paths and tracks through the estate are safe. Everyone knows that the lands belong to the Hintzens, and they know they always have; and they can't help knowing that the Hintzens are mean and hard. And then, everyone knows about Diamond Jim. But Diamond Jim keeps coming back. He's not like other folk who die and disappear when the bugs chew the crosses off their graves. It seems that when he came down the Courentyne he came to stay. All he needs is the hint of a full moon, and the kind of quiet that makes the leaves whisper in the guava trees, and he comes and sits out at Tarlojee, right up by the Big House, right up by the Hintzens. He's been known to sit and hum round by the kitchens, and he's been seen a few times by the still, but mostly he sits under the tree that old man Hintzen had him hanged on all those years ago, for daring to love his daughter, Miss Caroline.

*　　*　　*

That Caroline was wild, so they say. She didn't seem to have
the boiled water and metal for blood that Germans often do,
especially the old ones who've been out pushing back the jungle
for so many years they forget to be properly human. She didn't
even have the soft blood of the other rich folks with their
mixing of Spanish and Dutch. I've heard say that her mother
somehow put the eye of the hurricane in her little girl's eye,
and dead-hour sun in her blood and a goatskin drum in her
heart. Not even New Amsterdam on a Saturday night was wild
like her. She could make a bean stew into a banquet by laughing
over it. I think the reason why those two lovers didn't get
caught at first was because they were so wild no one could even
imagine what they were getting up to. The last person to know
it on the whole of Tarlojee was old man Hintzen himself, and
that was because he didn't know what imagination was let alone
possess any. So Miss Caroline and Diamond Jim spread two
years' harvest of diamond seed over the fields and in the sheds,
and for all I know in some of those empty rooms along the top
of the Big House where nobody ever goes.

It seems the good Lord didn't want to waste that fine seed,
and Miss Caroline started growing big under the red sash
round her middle.

Things like that will happen anywhere, but there's always
trouble when it happens to rich folk. People liked Diamond Jim,
though, they liked the style of him, the way he'd sit and hum
under the guava tree, with that diamond pin as big as a child's
eye fixing the bandanna round his neck. He had rum for
everyone, real rum and not even dregs. He had city stuff in his
pockets.

There were a lot of black men working in the fields, a lot of
black men going home dusty and grey with dirt. There were
some brown men too, all the shades of the earth: red, brown,
grey and I suppose we all looked much the same with our
trousers cut from the same bolt of cloth and tied round with
lengths of the same string. There were ways of being different,
mind you, in the shades of a bandanna round your neck, or the
tilt of a fibre hat, or even the cut of your shirt. But when it
came to who had what, we were all poor and we all had a lot of
mouths to feed and we used to joke that the cane hairs that

stuck in our backs were the iron filings old man Hintzen had
for spit because he talked so rough. Which made it only natural
that we should all admire Diamond Jim. He wasn't just black,
he shone. I swear his skin shone like the rings on his fingers
and the great stone at his throat. When he smiled he looked
like he could swallow up the whole of Tarlojee in that smile.
The kids used to say he could take anything and spit it out as
diamonds.

I don't know why we called him Jim, because his name, I
believe, was Walter. I don't know, either, who his family were.
He must have been somebody's son, and if they were about
they would surely have claimed him when he came striding
home with all his money and his confidence. Some say he must
have seen Miss Caroline somewhere in town and followed her
to Tarlojee and that was why he was there. But nobody knew
for sure. The fact is he came and stayed and when he started
messing with Miss Caroline everyone just waited and held their
breath for the deal that they liked that Diamond Jim, and the
dread they all had of old man Hintzen. Miss Caroline had so
much charm it was a weight for her to carry it about. It was as
though she was born knowing what was to happen to her. All
her high spirits seemed bottled up, and when she laughed it
came out like an explosion of locked-away things. She used to
say she liked the feel of the sun on the back of her neck. People
who work with cane can't understand a thing like that. She
liked to lie in the grass and sit on the prickly cane leaves and
she never had any fear of snakes. That's all I know about her
as a girl, just how strange she was and fanciful for the outdoors
and full of life and laughter. She must have really loved to be
alive to have lived on those twenty years in the tower with
nothing to see but the cracks of light through her boarded
window and the walls cracking as the years went by.

I've heard talk of people dying of laughter, and I think that's
just what killed that mismatched pair. When Caroline Hintzen
laughed it unsettled everything from the Big House down to
the river. It even made old men shudder and hold themselves,
and the little kids were scared. It had a strange effect. The sound
of it carried far and wide like the crashing of boulders along the

river bed in a flood. She was said to look like an angel and to laugh like a witch.

I don't know, and I don't expect I ever shall, who did bewitch the other out in the orchard under the noses of the whole world – and Tarlojee was a world in those days. Whoever it was began that crazy love affair, it soon reached such a pitch that it was just burning up worse than a cane fire with a following wind. There wasn't anyone left who didn't know about it. If they'd run away, who knows how far they would have got. Maybe they knew that not all the diamonds that Jim owned or even all the diamonds left in the hills could save that white girl and her big black lover. Maybe they could have made a dash into the Dutch country and hid out there, but black is black and Diamond Jim wasn't exactly inconspicuous anywhere. Then, maybe they thought they were invisible, protected somehow by the Lord himself in their great love from the vengeance of a man so cold he didn't even know that love existed.

It seems the lovers lasted longer than anyone dared hope for because of Hintzen's stubborn negation of the thing. While every night as the sun sank into the river and the stars signalled across the fields, Miss Caroline's frenzied laughter was like a flare to some and a map reference to others. No matter where they went, the whole working-force of Tarlojee and even her sisters knew where they were tumbling because of the manic braying that she did. There were times during the day, with no respect for the sun or the dead hours and no sense of a Sunday or rest, when the same thing would rise from field or hut as their love-making gathered pace.

Why, every day those two fools could have been caught. But time was suspended over Tarlojee while Miss Caroline nearly cloyed in the sweetness of her feelings for big Jim as he sat of an evening and hummed, with his back up against the grey bark of a guava tree, staring up at the stars with his eyes half-closed, passing messages it seemed from his big diamond up into the sky. Whatever it was he learned from that, it must have kept him there and vulnerable for all the months when he could have fled, alone or with the girl, and saved his life. He must have known that Hintzen would kill him when he knew. He must have known that, but didn't seem to care. Perhaps that's what the stars were telling him, that long after Hintzen died and his dust was spread, he, Diamond Jim, would still be sitting under his favourite tree, still humming his old tunes.

The rains came first, and they didn't look like the heaven-sent rain of other years because the storms kept coming down red. One night in July the bats died and everywhere around the house their thin furry bodies made a stretched grey layer like a carpet of tiny hidden bones. Later, it must have been in September, the yucca crop failed and the cane itself was slow to grow. Then it became apparent that Miss Caroline was growing in its stead. Some girls get pregnant and they can conceal the thing for months on end, but Miss Caroline wasn't just big, she was massive.

There were some good people out on Tarlojee around her, and some of them worked hard to cover up her tracks. But she herself seemed to have set her face against her fate and not to care, because she flaunted her great belly as though she was the proudest mother-to-be. And that went on until her father locked her up. I don't believe a mother would have let the old man drive her mad like he did. Maybe no mother could have saved poor Jim, but anyone with a heart could have helped Miss Caroline. It was her misfortune to be orphaned from any kindness in that house.

On that first night, Miss Caroline was locked up in the liquor room. It was always cold in there, windowless, with just a grid and a heavy bolted door. For a working man, that would be paradise, not punishment; but for the girl in love, used to a soft bed and company, it must have been hard. People said she called all through the night. Called and called, they said, with her great high voice winding through the cane and over the ridges.

Diamond Jim could have run away then, but he didn't. Instead, he stayed out all night long with his bright eyes glazed over, looking at the sky and humming fit to bust like a vibrating engine. Even the cicadas and the tree-frogs stopped eventually and there was just the wailing from inside the Big House and that one chord buzzing in Big Jim's throat. That was how he calmed her down. So the sun rose over the crest of the high fields, the ones that hillocked up beyond the dykes, with only the throbbing of Jim's voice to beckon it out of its sleep. He made the sun rise for him that day, willed it to set his stones in its gold because his own sun was going to set over Tarlojee before the day was out.

Eight o'clock saw the children passing by, scuttling past Jim as he sat waiting. They held the billy-cans close to their chests, and looked away, giggling shyly, and then looked back at the black giant they'd heard was going to die. They regrouped behind him, dawdling on the dust track, disappointed. He'd looked the same. He'd even smiled. Condemned men shouldn't smile. Dying was a serious matter.

People knew that Hintzen would never settle for a shooting. He'd want a proper lynching. So the workforce dwindled to the old and the boys that day, with a few women standing in for their men. All the strong ones stayed away drunk or feigning sickness, or just plain sick at the thought of helping to string up their hero. They couldn't do it. Well Hintzen never had trusted his men, he hadn't counted on them before and he didn't count on them then. He sent away to New Amsterdam in the night, and four big mulattos rode into the forecourt that morning, with hats and spurs and their eyes red with greed and rum.

Diamond Jim watched them coming and didn't stir. That was when the mystery happened. Those four mulattos swore that when they rode by, Jim's diamonds glistened and sparkled in the sun. But just moments later, when they went to get him, all his diamonds had gone. Now, no one passed by to take them, and the ground around him was dug and scratched and sieved and dug and no diamonds were ever found there . . . The mulattos said they thought Jim had hid the stones in his clothes, but after he died they stripped him bare and shredded the cloth. Nothing.

Before Jim died, Miss Caroline started calling again. But this time it wasn't just sounds and moans, it was straight words, 'Jim, don't ever leave me, Jim, Jim . . .'

Then he stood up, and his big voice gathered that was rarely heard except to sing, and he called back to her, 'Caro, honey, I ain't going nowhere.'

The man never spoke again, as such. I don't really know

what happened next. Some say they cast the rope around his neck and hanged him but he wouldn't die, so those four riders shot him through. Some say they had to shoot him to get the noose on him at all. One thing's for sure, though, the diamonds never were found. All down the years, vandals have been turning over Jim's bones to see if he swallowed those diamonds, but no good ever came of it, and no stones were ever found.

And no good ever came from hanging Jim. Before the year was out, the four mulattos who did it were jinxed, and they drank themselves to their ruin, haunted, they said, by the big smile on his face. And Hintzen? Even Hintzen wished he'd waited with his hanging, because four months later, when Miss Caroline gave birth to a huge grey baby girl, he wanted to kill Jim all over again and there was nothing left of him to hurt. Being a Christian, he couldn't destroy the child but he took her away one night and returned a week later without her. That's what the towns were like, they'd swallow up the living and the dead. The baby must have been two weeks old then, and already turned as black as the man who made her.

After the baby went, Hintzen shifted his daughter into the stone tower, and that was when Miss Caroline started some serious calling. She'd got the idea that all she had to do was cry out hard enough and Big Jim would answer her. Well, Miss Caroline stayed in that tower for twenty years calling out across the cane fields for the man she loved. She never gave up in all that time trying to summon him back to her. It must have been about a year later that her tired sad voice cracked and turned into bouts of crazy laughter.

Her call had come to be a part of Tarlojee, like the animal call of the bush, and the keening of circling birds. It carried through the lanes between the sugar canes, and it settled in the daubed mud on the huts. People seemed to stir it in with their bean stew and corn. The dregs of her wailing sat with the pineapple rinds and fermented in pitchers of water. Jim's name was everywhere.

A lot happens in a lifetime, and things get forgotten. Details blur and disappear, and facts merge until only a few events stand out. Sometimes they're not events at all, just passing images, and sometimes they're so powerful they stop your blood from running for a while. That was how the laughter sounded after a year of tears. To hear Miss Caroline braying again chilled all of Tarlojee to the bone. It was her mating call, and, I suppose, it was all part of what held Jim to her because the night she started rattling her wild laugh about, Diamond Jim came back. He had his diamonds on again – the rings and the big one at his throat that communed with the stars. He sat all night under his guava tree and he hummed, a loud throbbing hum, and although no one touched him – because no one dared – he was there, smiling like he could, as though he knew something special, with his big teeth shining out and almost competing with the eye-diamond, the diamond that started it all, that gave him his name, and made him a myth.

A lot of nights have passed since then, and a lot of years. Miss Caroline has been dead now for a long time, but Big Jim still sits out sometimes, waiting, and he still hums. And, although he's never done any of us any harm, there's no one goes down to the ruins of the Big House on a full moon. The kids nowadays laugh about it too, but there's not one of them eats guavas in Tarlojee or ever hums like a lost tune finding its way out of the sugar cane.

The Lady Gardener

Nobody at the nursing home liked to bother Gladys. She had come and gone now in a haze of pent-up rage for seven years. She knew her way around the corridors as well as any member of staff, and she could always make her way, unaccompanied, past the Macmillan and Nightingale wards, past the side room where the girl with the twisted face who was no more than a torso tucked into the top part of the bed lay unvisited, and on to the room where her own daughter Sally lay and had lain for more than half her life. It was eight years since the car had hit her, but the verdict was always the same: brain-dead, and hitched to the tubes and drips and bags and the yards of plastic that were all that Sally had now for her adolescence.

Gladys herself was soothed by these visits to her daughter. She fitted them in whenever she could. She would sit for hours behind the half-blinds silently discussing all the minor worries that had come to beset her in her early middle age. There were slugs on her borders again, and Simpson was behind with the mowing, the front brake-discs were going on the Daimler. Sally was the perfect listener.

At three o'clock exactly, Gladys rose to leave. She had a small travelling bag with her in worn red leather, and a summer coat. She was well dressed for the small Norfolk village where she lived, but not strikingly so for London, and, standing as she did at a mere five foot four, with her rather snubbed features and her dull olive skin, she made no effort to be striking. In fact, she thought, she owed half her success in her job to the very unobtrusiveness of her appearance. Pausing between the massive gate-posts of the clinic to take a last look at Sally's window, Gladys certainly didn't look anything out of the ordinary. But then, as she herself had explained at her interview, it isn't what you look like, it's what you feel like and how capably you work that counts, and Gladys just happened to be the best.

She caught the three-thirty train to Liverpool Street, and drifted through East Anglia, with an open book on her knee, reflecting on the sequence of events that had led her to where she was. She had become so English over the years, with her tweeds and her Burberry, and her place on the flower-rota at the church, that she often forgot that she wasn't. She wasn't, actually, even European, but she had married on a lie, and the lie had stuck, and with every passing year it seemed more and more pointless to enlighten her husband. Alec probably wouldn't have believed her anyway. For all his merits, he didn't have a very vivid imagination. So he thought she was born German, because she had once had German papers for a few years, and he didn't realize now, on the eve of their trip to Caracas, that for Gladys this would really mean going home. She had been born there in the shanty town that spilled down the hill-slopes into the city in a wave of delinquency and ungathered debris.

Gladys had always had a distaste for the squalor of her birth. Her own mother had run away and left her to fend for herself in the one-room hut that couldn't keep out the rain, let alone rats or intruders. Even then, Gladys's plainness had been like a shield. She had always been too small, and then, later, too ordinary, to bother with. She was fourteen when she ran away to join the guerrillas. And by the time she was fifteen, she had earned herself the name of *La Loba*, the she-wolf. For three years she had never moved without a weapon, never slept without a gun. And then, one by one, there seemed to be fewer battles, fewer victories, fewer people and less fun, and *La Loba* decided to become Gladys again. So she made her last skirmish into Valera, and stole a knitted two-piece in lightweight cotton, and a pair of stockings and some smart lace-up shoes. She swapped identity cards and papers with a German girl called Gladys Lorenz, student, who had come to join the guerrillas; as Gladys Lorenz she set sail for Hamburg, and from Hamburg took the train to Berlin.

That was where Alec came in. Alec was a financial adviser for Shell. He was thirty-eight, and at five foot ten he didn't tower too hopelessly over her. He had a good job and a small private income and he was the kindest man she had ever met. Alec was totally incompetent in the everyday running of his life, and he seemed to find, in Gladys, the perfect bride. However much his work took him away from Berlin, he would return, again and again, to the spotless flat on the Tempelhofer Ufer where Gladys lived. Within the year, they were married. They never agreed about anything, except the garden, and, either despite or maybe because of this, they were very happy together.

From Liverpool Street Gladys took the tube to Piccadilly and walked down to Fortnum's to meet Alec for tea. England was to play Scotland at Wembley, and the crowds in the street were unusually large. Gladys became quite anonymous in a crowd. She was only someone to be reckoned with one to one. At tea she ate three different kinds of cake and then felt too full to talk.

'You'll get fat,' Alec told her.

But she was already just that little bit too much overweight to be able to do anything about it without a great deal of effort, so she didn't bother. Besides which, she felt a sense of heightened excitement at the thought of returning to Caracas after so many years, even if it was only to be for the three days of their trip, and she was especially pleased at the thought of closing an option while she was there. It made her hungry.

Gladys looked out across the neighbouring tables and fixed her stare on a woman with a pink floppy hat and far too much lipstick who was pinching a thin nervous boy while he ate, threatening him under her breath through clenched teeth. Gladys felt her anger rise. Alec paid and got up to go.

'We're late,' he said, apologetically.

Gladys gathered her bags together and followed him to the door. As she passed the pink hat, she paused to say:

'If you pinch that child again, I shall report you.'

'What a woman!' Alec said with disgust as he held open the swing doors.

At Heathrow, their luggage was waiting for them. Gladys always sent it on a few hours ahead. Alec took a vast number of belongings with him wherever he went, and the more he travelled the more he seemed to want to have what was most precious near him. In this he had grown decidedly more neurotic since Sally's accident, taking endless pieces of stone and china, and great chunks of the library, packed in layers of wool and tissue. He had never been so close to Gladys as he was now, in gratitude for her efficiency. He liked her to travel with him wherever he went. Just being near to her calmed his nerves.

Gladys found flying very conducive to thought. She unclipped her seat-belt and lay back, remembering, as she did every day of her life, the accident of eight years ago. She remembered how the car had careered through their village at fifty miles an hour, and how Sally, on the pavement on her bicycle, had seen it and stopped, and how even so it had swerved into her and thrown her back into their own garden like a clot of compost. Further on, the car had stopped and a woman driver had staggered out. Not hurt, but drunk, so drunk she could hardly stand, and she had come and breathed whisky over the hedge. She had come crying for forgiveness.

Gladys remembered the long vigils at the National Hospital, four months of purgatory on the danger list, and then the long years without any hope. She remembered the trial, and the nine-month sentence and the warning. And she remembered how the woman had wept in court, and the judge had suspended the sentence, 'because,' he said, 'the remorse was punishment enough'. He had thanked God that Sally was still alive. But Sally was brain-dead, and only seven, and nearly as tall as Gladys even then, and she would lie for seven years like a dead heron around her mother's throat. Alec had aged and become more obsessive, carting his hobbies from port to port with him, while Gladys planned her revenge.

Gladys waited a year before she took action, and when the time came she took great pains to make the murder look like suicide. She was surprised to find, after ten years of coffee mornings and tombola, with what ease she could still kill. She was even more surprised to discover that beyond the vengeance, the real pleasure had come in the challenge and the act itself.

She returned to her garden with her appetite for killing whetted as never before.

Four days later, she read an advertisement in one of the Sunday papers: 'Palm Beach sponsor seeks lady gardeners for unusual work. Applicants must not be squeamish about killing slugs', and then there was an address in Percy Street. It was the bit about the slugs that really interested Gladys. It gave her an inkling of what they were after. But it wasn't until the interview that she fully realized what the job was to be. She was interviewed by a tall American woman called Cynthia who introduced herself as being 'into pest control'. She claimed to be compiling a paper on women's attitudes to extermination techniques, but gradually, during the course of that first inter view, and then subsequent ones, she explained her true predicament.

'I work for these two very nice old ladies in Palm Beach,' Cynthia had said, 'but they have a problem.'

Gladys had decided to say as little as possible until she learnt more where she stood.

'They're not happy with the way things happen,' Cynthia had explained. 'They think the world is losing its balance.

'They like to think of themselves as owning a garden,' Cynthia continued, 'and they would like to do a bit of weeding, just routine pest control.'

Gladys listened, delighted by what she heard.

'I did a little research on you, Mrs . . .'

'Gladys,' Gladys interrupted.

'Gladys,' Cynthia repeated in her deep, soothing psy chiatrist's voice. 'And I know about your little girl. Now I believe that women have a great role to play in life, and I believe that a capable woman is the most capable being there is, but sometimes,' she paused, lowering her eyes with almost religious dismay, 'they get away with murder.'

Gladys nodded, and Cynthia concluded where she had begun, 'Back in Palm Beach, they don't like it. Now I've done some recruiting in New York, and I've found myself a great secretary, but I can't find the women who can get out there and actually kill the slugs.'

'I think you need me,' Gladys told her.

Cynthia eyed her carefully. She decided that Gladys had hidden qualities.

'Tell me about yourself,' Cynthia suggested, and Gladys unfolded a little of her past.

Ten days later she had got the job, but she insisted on one condition, that she was to be the only person to deal with the slugs.

'Well, I was really envisaging five or six,' Cynthia told her.

'Then I'll work six times as hard,' Gladys said firmly. And she had, for six years, travelling under Alec's wing, she worked her way through the old ladies' lists, eliminating the women who had 'got away with murder'. Some of them were public figures, most of them were not, but they had all caused suffering and been left untouched by the law. When Gladys had asked, 'Why only women?' Cynthia had replied, with her favourite opening phrase:

'Research has shown, that nobody keeps the balance where women are concerned, so we're just going where we are needed.'

The plane was landing at Madrid, just a transit-lounge affair before the long leg to Caracas. Gladys took her book and opened it somewhere in the middle. It was her flight book, Thackeray this time, read in bouts and snatches between take-offs and sleeping, worn open on her knees more as a mask to ward off conversation than for anything else. Not that Alec ever talked much when they were travelling. He was always mildly airsick and always worried that he might get worse, so he monitored his stomach, and kept himself to himself.

Gladys was thinking about the two old ladies, sitting out on their piazza in Palm Beach, Florida, or taking coffee in the Waldorf Astoria in New York, or visiting their daughters in East Hampton. One of them, Mildred, was wheelchair-bound, and propelled by a private nurse; Lilian, the other, was very deaf, and they were both watched over by a private army. They were the widows of oil magnates and they had spent their married lives listening to the latest figures in the Dow-Jones index.

Both the old ladies were immensely bored and immensely rich, and as they had come to know each other better, over the years, Gladys could see how they had gradually come to take the law into their own hands. She could imagine their satisfaction in feeling that they were coming down like the wrath of God through the instrument of herself, their lady gardener. The only drawback in the whole set-up was their zeal. Their lists were getting longer and longer, and Cynthia had had to extend her capacity to that of moderator, and censor their slugs. Mixed in with the criminals were the names of those who had done nothing worse than criticize Mildred's make-up, or whisper words that Lilian could not hear. The old ladies were growing vicious.

Gladys always did things herself anyway. It was just the way she was. She always went round the garden after Simpson, her gardener, had finished, redoing little jobs to her own satisfaction. And she always checked out the women she was to get close to; before she killed them, she made sure that they really had done what they were accused of doing. She allowed no extenuating circumstances. She didn't want to know why the woman who ran her Sally down was drunk. For Gladys, carelessness and thoughtlessness were failures, and failure was guilt. It was not her job to be fair, merely to restore a sense of balance. She would have had no more thought of putting the slugs on her herbaceous border on trial before baiting them than she would have had of trying the slugs on her lists. They were eating her delphiniums, and they had to go.

Gladys slept a little on the plane, and woke up feeling dishevelled and out of sorts. She pulled her skirt straight, and made her way to the bathroom at the back of the cabin. In her toilet-bag she had a miniature tooth-mug which she filled with tap-water, disregarding the usual warnings about its undrinkable quality. She carefully prepared herself a glass of liver salts, drinking them while they were still fizzy. Gladys's stomach and liver could have been galvanized they were so strong, but she liked the taste of the salts, and always carried a tin of them in her handbag, together with an enormous jar of aspirin, her make-up, her flight book, and a minute container of Mace nerve gas made to look just like a lipstick. The Mace often came in very useful. Cynthia would probably have to get her another container after this trip, she thought.

Gladys hadn't followed an option for five and a half weeks, and it made her rather edgy. The killing had come to be what drink or cigarettes were to her friends, halfway between a pleasure and an addiction. Every three months a new list would be made up and handed to her by Cynthia, who in turn would have liaised and haggled with the old ladies to come to the names that stood. Gladys would take the whole list, like so many options, picking out slugs as she saw them and not as they wanted them. The old ladies specifically didn't want publicity, they just wanted success. Gladys had a way of making most of the deaths look like suicide, and a way of waiting. The woman she was after in Caracas had been on one of her lists for four years.

Cynthia had a fair-sized file on her. She was called Maria Perez, she was twenty-nine, beautiful, rich and spoiled. Four years ago she had been the mistress of the registrar of a children's clinic. One night when he was on duty, he had left the building to have dinner with Maria Perez, leaving her telephone number in case of an emergency. Before driving to her house in an elegant suburb of Caracas known as Valle Arriba, he had locked the children into their wards. During his absence, a fire had broken out at the clinic, and no one had been able to reach him. The evidence at the inquest had caused a scandal.

Maria Perez took the three telephone calls herself that came from the clinic, and each time she denied that the registrar was in her house.

'But there is no one in charge here,' a distraught nurse had told her.

'Then you be in charge,' Maria Perez had said, and hung up.

Later, the same nurse had tried again.

'The firemen haven't come, and we can't unlock the doors to get the children out.'

'It's none of my business,' Maria Perez had told her, 'let them climb out of the windows.'

But the windows were barred, and before any firemen could break through the doors and fumes, sixteen children died of asphyxiation. Two months later, the registrar shot himself, the enquiry was closed, and Maria Perez walked away from the courtroom smiling.

Gladys had a cutting from a recent society magazine. It read: 'A Day in the Life of Maria Perez. Every morning, at half past ten, Maria takes her adorable chihuahua, Fifi, for a walk by her fabulous mansion in Valle Arriba . . .' That was really all Gladys needed to know. This time it would be so easy that she would have qualms about keeping her pay. Whenever this happened, she donated her wages to The Latin People's Trust for Endangered Species, a charity that was dear to her heart.

Gladys rubbed some complimentary almond cream into her face and then looked at herself in the mirror. She knew that she wasn't pretty, but nobody could say that she didn't have a pleasant face. And but for Sally, she reflected, no one would say that she didn't have a pleasant life, lots of free travel and a lovely husband. The 'Fasten your seat belt' sign came up, and Gladys swung her way back to her seat, feeling lucky and smiling: even her job, that was so much a part of her, didn't take her time away from Alec or the garden, or her visits to Sally or her entertaining.

The plane landed on its nose, as they so often do in South America, and then bumped and thumped to a standstill with an alarming chorus of shrieks and cries from the passengers and crew.

'Thank God it's stopped,' Alec said, after they had screeched to a halt. 'Are you all right, poppet?'

'Yes, I'm fine, thanks. How about you?'

'Well, I'm all right, but I'm damn glad I didn't bring any of my Tiffany this time.'

Later he asked, 'Where are we staying?'

'At a place called the Tamanaco. It looked a bit like something out of *Star Wars* on the brochure, but I think it'll be quite fun.

'By the way,' she added, casually, 'I think I'll do a bit of shopping tomorrow morning.'

Alec squeezed her hand, 'You and your shopping,' he said indulgently, 'wherever we go, you've always got a bit of shopping to do.'

*   *   *

There was a hired car waiting for them at the desk, and they had a drive of over fifty kilometres from the airport at Maiquetía to the city itself. Gladys always did the driving, and they lurched from side to side of their hired Mustang all along the coast road, swerving and swingtailing through the thick traffic to the hotel. Alec arrived looking rather ashen, his knuckles aching from gripping the seat.

'Are you all right, darling?' Gladys asked him as she helped him from the car.

'Yes,' he said, shakily, 'I must say, I was rather worried about how you'd manage with those maniacs, but in the end, I was more scared about falling over the cliff.'

'I wouldn't let anything happen to you, Alec,' Gladys said reassuringly. 'Anyway, I'm starving.'

Gladys found dinner and all its trappings one of her great pleasures in life. She had second and third helpings of the guasacaca and then ploughed her way through the following courses, ending up with a sugary fudge so sweet it cloyed.

Alec said, 'I don't know how you can eat that muck.'

'It's rather nice, actually,' Gladys told him.

He pulled a face.

'Well, you eat snails,' she said.

'But I like snails,' he protested.

Gladys looked at him sadly.

'And anyway,' he added hastily, 'I don't eat them now that we're always together.'

But Gladys had lost the last of her appetite, and was lost in thought. She had an ampoule of coramine in her handbag, which was in itself a cardio-accelerator, but she had shaken up a little cocktail with a couple of other drugs, and the mixture was very nasty. As an intramuscular injection, it would work in a matter of seconds. Alec was looking tired, so they went to bed early.

Next morning, Gladys took the hired Mustang from the hotel car park, and picked her way in and out of the traffic jams to Valle Arriba, where the millionaires' mansions and the golf-course made a pleasant change from the chaos of the city below them. It was ten-fifteen when she parked the car. She had taken great pains with her dress that morning, and she was looking Caraqueñan smart. In a city obsessed with fashion, she knew that the well-dressed were a class apart. Two cars raced past her, chasing each other down the precarious slope. She ignored them, and prepared a disposable hypodermic syringe with 3 c.c. of her mixture. It was ten-twenty-two. She put the Cellophane wrapper in her pocket, together with the needle cover, then she put her gloves on, and waited. At ten-thirty she was still waiting, and she was still waiting at ten-forty.

It was only at ten-fifty-two that she heard the click of a woman's heels coming down the hill, strained forward. Gladys was two hundred and fifty yards from the entrance to Maria Perez's home, waiting behind a crag of rock that gave directly on to the road. The first thing to come into her field of vision was a beige chihuahua. Gladys was crouching at the dog's level, and she gave it no more than a scent of Mace. The dog passed out. Behind it came Maria Perez, distraught at her pet's collapse. Gladys had moved back, and now she moved forward.

'Permiso,' she said, pushing forward, 'I am a vet,' and, as she spoke, she plunged her unsheathed needle through the turquoise silk of Maria Perez's flying suit. Then she stepped back again, bent the needle double, put it in her pocket and walked back to her car. It was ten-fifty-five and Gladys was at the wheel of the Mustang, cruising down past the CADA supermarket, and back to the city itself.

By lunch-time, laden with shopping, Gladys was feeling ready for food. She had decided to eat in a German tea shop known as El Chicken, which was an abbreviation for El Chicken Bar. It had once been a gathering-place for intellectuals, poets, actors, idealists and hangers-on. Now, as she looked around her, she saw no one she knew or even vaguely recognized. But the cakes were still as good, and on the pavement, stretching out from either side of the awnings, the wide avenue of Sabana Grande ranged from official splendour at one end to the heart of gangland crime at the other.

Gladys remembered the gangland Caracas, sewn up into compartments on the four corners of the adjoining streets that met like the tines of a fork at the junction below her. They called the top corner the Bank of Switzerland. Finance, drugs, prostitution and homosexuals each had their own niche. But Gladys's tourist instincts were at a low par. She would rather get back to Alec, who might have finished his meeting and be missing her.

She drove back to the Tamanaco Hotel, to find Alec lying down and upset about something.

'What's up?' she asked him, dropping her shopping at the door of their room.

'I'm terribly sorry, poppet,' he said, 'something has just cropped up, and I'm going to have to go to a summit in Egypt.'

'You poor thing.'

'Could you bear to come too?' he asked pathetically. 'At such short notice?'

'Of course I will, Alec, you know I always come with you now.'

'Egypt is such a ghastly place to do business in, all flies and dark glasses. There will be one day in London between flights, but we may as well stay up.'

'I think I'll nip down and see Sally, actually, I don't like to leave her too long,' Gladys said.

Back in Norfolk, at the clinic, Gladys sat with her hand on the counterpane of her daughter's bed. In her bag she had a copy of *El Nacional*, which she had bought in the foyer of the Tamanaco on her way out. On the middle pages the obituaries hung, draped in black trails of paper ribbon. Four of them were given over to Maria Perez, 'who had died suddenly of a coronary near her home in Valle Arriba'. She had been a society figure, a member of what they called 'el high'. The details were all there. Gladys folded up the newspaper and tucked it into her bag, where it lay beside the file on her next option, a middle-aged American woman who lived on a top-security ranch in Wyoming. She had operated for fifteen years what was coming to be the largest heroin ring in the Western USA. 'Research had shown' that she would be in Cairo, supervising the purity of her wares. If only, Gladys thought, this new option had dedicated herself to cancer research with the same fervour that she gave to narcotics, she could probably have found a cure by now. Cynthia had said, 'You can't miss her, she has a lavender rinse and fly-away glasses,' and Gladys was cheered by these details.

She wished that she had time to go back and see the house. At least she could look forward to it later, tea in the red room, and a walk in the garden. Sally hadn't moved, wouldn't and never could. But Gladys smiled at her. She stayed for half an hour, talking to herself, and then she rose to go. She was wearing the new hat she had bought in Caracas, but she rammed it into her shopping bag before she left. All the way down to the car park she could see the chewed leaves of the flowers. According to Simpson, it was a bad year for slugs.

The Green Boy

Antonio didn't like the child to be talked of as 'the green boy'. To him, he was always El Capino, his son. On the second day he had sent the child down in advance, led like a sick lizard by his sister. He had hoped that the Doña would cure him. He watched from above as his daughter, Mary, picked her way over the stream and weeds to the courtyard of the Big House. El Capino was his favourite, but Capino was sick.

Mary had crossed the bridge, following the willow-lined track past the machine house and mill and on through the gates and garden to the Doña's house. She tried to leave Capino by the barn, but he clung to her, frightened to stay alone. A bad man lived in the gallery of the barn. He shrank back from its double doors. He didn't want to be left. Mary pushed him back firmly against the wall, whispering, 'Just wait a minute, Capino, I'll be back. Hush, and the bad man won't get you.'

Capino leaned heavily against the wall, unreassured by these words, but too limp to move. He was five years old. He was in trouble and very afraid. Mary ran into the yard and called, 'Doña, Doña, where are you?'

A voice answered, 'I'm upstairs, I'll come.'

Lydia, as the Doña was called, appeared, glad to see Mary. She always liked to see the girl and her little brother. Lydia was new on the hacienda, and a foreigner, and the two children kept her company, childless as she was, and they kept her informed about all that happened in the valley. Mary had a genius for never coming empty-handed. She would bring strange flowers for the garden, or a clothful of rose-scented plums. She brought snail shells and seeds, or mottled beans to pod. There was hardly a day when Mary didn't come with some little offering or surprise. So that when she said, 'I've brought something to show you,' Lydia said, 'Thank you,' without really thinking.

Then Mary brought her brother forward and stood him in the courtyard in the sun. His pale skin was green, as were his limp hands by his sides. The whites of his eyes were marbled green and even his fair hair, which gave him the name of Capino, which means blond, was spiky green in the sun. Lydia was at a loss. He seemed so dull and lifeless that she reached out to touch him to see if he was real.

Mary said, 'Mother says to help him.'

Lydia looked from the girl to the sad little boy, wondering how he could possibly have been dyed so thoroughly.

'What is it?' she asked.

'He's taken a paper,' Mary said.

'A paper of what?' asked Lydia.

'Will he die?' Mary answered simply.

The implications of the boy's colour crossed Lydia's mind for the first time. She wondered if it could be some generalized gangrene, but it clearly wasn't. There was no smell and the boy's skin was not a dark rotten colour; it was clearer, like bean leaves or the tendrils of a vine. El Capino was hauntingly strange, he was very definitely green, more green even than the bloated underbelly of a dead fish. His colour and listlessness were reptilian.

Mary was asking, 'Will he die?'

'Loosen the wheel,' Lydia ordered, and the girl ran away, relieved to have something to do.

'Will I die?' Capino whimpered, his green fingers clawing at her skirt. 'Will I die?' he pleaded, echoing his sister's words. She tried to reassure him and then left him standing in the yard while she beat together egg whites and water. She could hear the slow clanking of the wheel, and then the rumble as it gathered speed. Its empty rumbling, out of harvest time, was the signal for all and sundry to gather at the Big House. It was only ever used in emergencies. Its sound was loud enough to carry through all the lands of the hacienda. Its rush and thud began to ring through the valley, tolling alarm. She covered the child's head with a towel.

'Will I die?' he murmured.

'You'll be all right,' she said. 'Drink this, it will help you.'

His voice continued as monotonous as the mill wheel turning, 'Will I die, will I die?'

Lydia realized that the boy could neither hear nor understand her any more. She left him standing. She could see him turning to the colour of weathered bronze, and he looked slightly absurd with the cloth on his head to shield him from the sun. She fetched Mary back.

'Make him drink this,' she said, handing her the glass of egg and water. Mary held the glass to his dry lips and tipped; it spilled slimy down his chin and chest, but he swallowed a little, shuddering.

High on the hill, Antonio had heard the wheel turn that day, and the idle clanking of the mill had frightened him. He knew from long experience that the thud and clatter of the massive wheel always announced bad news. It had called him down for over sixty years now. And that day it turned to spread the news of his son's disease. He had hoped for a miracle from the Doña, but none had come. Antonio thought that if a miracle would come to save this child of his old age, he would even believe in God. But then the mill wheel had turned, sounding her failure and its own alarm across the hills, summoning everyone to the Big House.

He saw people begin to stir and stop in their tracks. As the noise continued, he saw them heading for the Big House and the courtyard and his son. By the time he reached the gates, quite a crowd had gathered. They stopped him as he went in, quizzing him, but Antonio was in no mood to speak, and he brushed past them to the house itself.

Lydia said, 'I'm sorry, Antonio, but we'll have to take him into town . . . to the hospital.'

Antonio turned to fetch the lorry. The very word 'hospital' was like death itself to him. He backed the old lorry to as near the courtyard as he could get, while Mary and Lydia carried El Capino to him. The workers at the gates craned forward to see, starting back in disbelief. Lydia asked them to take care of the house in her absence, and thanked them for coming so promptly. As the lorry lurched on its way to town, the crowd behind them began to disperse. They seemed disappointed by the lack of action.

Lydia watched the fields of sugar cane stretching out on either side and rising into the thickly wooded hills. All the different greens seemed to glare forward that day, comparing themselves to El Capino's vivid skin. He was the colour of lettuce leaves and young banana palms, of marsh grass and ripe passion fruits. His cheekbones and knuckles seemed almost as dark as the cane itself and the convolvulus that grew around it. And his thin eyebrows were like dull lichen. El Capino himself didn't heed or even hear his sister's words, or bother that she fussed and buttoned him. Twice he sicked up the albuminous water transformed to pond weed by his poisoned stomach. The mess slid on the floor of the truck in a deep green mass.

Lydia half-sensed that there was something to hide. They were still five miles from the hospital. Antonio was driving, and his son was saying: 'Will I die will I die?' all rolled into one.

She knew that someone was going to ask, and it may as well be her, so she plucked up the courage and said, 'What has he taken, Antonio?'

Antonio looked away and murmured, 'Copper sulphate.'

'What?'

'Copper sulphate,' he repeated.

'But that's rat poison,' she said. 'How did he come by it?'

'It was in the chemist's paper.'

'How much did he take?'

'All of it.'

Lydia was silent. She hardly dared ask how Capino could have swallowed such a quantity of poison.

'But the taste,' she argued. 'It's even disguised for rats.'

'He didn't like it,' Antonio faltered.

Capino's head had lolled against the glass, he was gripping his stomach as though disembowelled under his torn shirt, and he was whispering to the window: 'Will I die, will I die?'

'When did he take it?' Lydia asked.

'Last night,' Antonio answered and his face was blank with grief.

'Why didn't you bring him to me before?'

'We were afraid,' he said simply.

Lydia brooded as the lorry jogged along. Capino repeated his sing-song to the glass. He was sick once more before he fainted.

'What will you say at the hospital, Doña?'

'What will you say, Antonio?'

'I'll say that it was an accident.'

'Then so will I,' she said.

The lorry pulled up outside the hospital. It looked like an open-air concert. Row upon row of women and children sat in folding chairs surrounded by siege-like quantities of provisions. They only ever came in desperation and they had little hope of recovery. To them the hospital was a grim last resort. Nothing that happened there surprised them. It ate into their families, reducing their numbers with its neglect. At one time or another they had all heard the standard 'come back in three months'. It was like the ducking of witches. Those who lasted three months could usually last more, and those who died in the interim wouldn't need that later appointment. However, some cases always defied delay, and the green boy was one of them. Antonio gathered up his son and pushed his way past the trollied heaps of stab wounds, gun wounds and burns. Then he carried him on past the waiting queues and a murmur rose up behind him. A green boy had come down from the hills. A nurse came up to Capino, she took a look at him and asked a few questions. Then an orderly wheeled him away in the direction of the dressing-room and the stomach-pump. A trickle of brown blood was running down his leg.

Antonio and Lydia were left alone in the corridor. Lydia had never been in the hospital before and she didn't know what to do.

'He hasn't got a chance like this,' Antonio said. 'The only way to survive this place is to use your influence. Have all the wards paged, Doña, use your name. It will bring some good doctors to us. There have to be people with a special interest in a patient here, because if they don't die of neglect they just die of the general disorder. And the children's ward is the worst of the lot.'

Antonio had taken off his hat and he was fingering the brim, nervously. His eyes were slightly bleary from the residue of years of direct midday sun, and drink, and old age edging over them.

'Ramón,' he continued, 'who works in the mill, had a little boy in here last year, before you came. He was just a baby. They couldn't deal with his fever at home, so they had to bring him in. It was pneumonia. The doctors wouldn't let them stay, but Ramón came back early the next morning, and they told him he'd died of the fever. Well, he had in a way, you see, they'd put the baby on a great high bed and not bothered to draw up the side, so he rolled over with his fever and broke his head. Ramón said they hadn't even bothered to wipe away the blood from the floor; and all the bones were broken in his face.'

Lydia squeezed Antonio's sleeve and then stood up. At the desk she just gave her name and address, twice, to make sure it had sunk in. Within minutes the gloomy lobby seemed to come to life. One of the trolleys was wheeled off to the morgue, and a general air of activity bristled about the place. Notes were being taken about Capino's case. Soon Capino himself reappeared, greener than ever, swamped in a regulation gown. He had a drip rigged in to his arm, and a bag hanging from the edge of the trolley collecting his trickle of poisoned urine. He had come round, and was wheeled through the arch of expectant doctors, as though through a guard of honour, and as he passed, he left a trail of questions like confetti.

'Will I die? Will I die? Will I die?'

Lydia recognized one or two of the men there, and entrusted the sick child to their care. Mary would be able to stay by his bedside while she and Antonio returned for the child's mother. The armed guard at the door was asking Antonio, 'Who bought the poison?'

'I did,' said Lydia firmly and followed this statement with such a hard look that the guard merely stood to attention and forebore to ask the other questions that he had in mind.

They rode the bumpy journey back together and neither of them spoke. They took the lorry along the dirt track of the plantation to the foot of the hill where Antonio lived, and then they left it to go on foot. Lydia felt herself come of age in the mile's distance that they climbed that day. Antonio spoke to her most of the way.

'We don't like doctors here,' he began. 'We don't trust them.'

They walked on a little, and then he continued: 'There's a witch-doctor who lives over the hill, Doña, who has a way with ailments. I've known him all my life, and he has been a help to us many times. Some of his cures are famous hereabouts.'

'And is that where you took Capino?' Lydia asked.

'Yes, he'd been ailing all year. He's my favourite, you know, and it hurt me to see him pine. This witch-doctor used to be a simple man like me. I had faith in him. There is little left to have faith in.'

Antonio strode ahead, jabbing the path bitterly with his woven shoes.

'But even he has changed now,' he continued. 'He has taken to writing down his remedies. He has grown too proud to speak his cures any more.'

Lydia looked at Antonio's gaunt face. He was labouring to tell his tale. And she listened, following his words as best she could.

'So when he sent his medicine for Capino's stomach pains, he wrote it down on a scrap of paper.'

Lydia listened in silence. She knew that Antonio couldn't read, and she realized that he must have bought the poison himself and forced it down the child.

'Didn't they ask what it was for at the chemist's?' she asked.

'Yes,' he said, 'I told them it was for the hacienda, and they let me have it. They must have known,' he murmured. 'They must have thought it was for bait.'

Lydia felt for him as never before. There was nothing she could do or say to ease his pain, so she just let him talk on.

'You see,' he explained, 'you don't expect medicine to taste nice. When Capino wouldn't take it, we held him down, and I made him drink it. Some of the powder was like little granules and I crushed them up for him.

'We thought he would stop crying soon, but when he cried all through the night we were afraid. The women said it was the evil eye, but I knew that it was the paper.

'From the day they built a box of old fruit crates to bury my mother in, denying her a proper coffin, I have known what shame is. But I never thought I'd live to see the day when I'd kill my own boy.'

They had reached the bend in the path that curled around the dead lemon tree in Antonio's yard. He finished what he was saying almost hurriedly.

'The witch doctor made a mistake, Doña. He's not used to fancy names. I don't know what he meant to write . . .'

Lydia interrupted him. She was furious.

'I know what he meant to write,' she hissed. 'He meant to write Epsom Salts. But, like you said,' she added savagely, 'he's not used to fancy names, and he must have written copper for magnesium sulphate.' She paused. 'And now it's tearing through your Capino. What are you going to do about it, Antonio?'

Antonio sucked in his cheeks.

'I can see you think I should denounce him,' he said, 'but he's one of us, and he's the only help we've got. And this boy, Capino, was all I had, and now I must tell his mother to go and watch him die.'

Antonio stared down at the ground, and Lydia felt too sick to speak, so they both just steered their way through the milk tins of geraniums and the fallen pods of Antonio's yard.

Over the next five days they went to and fro, Antonio aging daily, and Lydia doing everything within her power to save the child. And it was then that she realized for the first time the extent and the limitations of this power. The blood bank was filled up by radio appeals for El Capino's Rhesus negative transfusions. He was given every medical aid available in the hospital, where ultra-modern equipment and neglect bulged side by side. Each day new lengths were reached in treatment and diagnosis. Ambulances were brought and cancelled, a fully-equipped military plane stood by to move the child to Maracaibo, if necessary. Plasma was flown in in frozen containers. His old kidneys were linked to a kidney machine, his heart and lungs to life-support, and a transplant surgeon was hired to take the case on at the military hospital. But the little plastic bag that trailed by Capino's side defied all efforts. It slowly filled with a darker and darker blood, until a thick black paste was all that

came. And the child's thin voice calling out to the host of staff
that towered over his bed asked,
    'Will I die? Will I die?'
and seemed almost to mock their sudden concern.

On the fifth day, he did die, and his bowels were removed as is
the custom, and in respect of his patron, he was sewn up neatly
and filled with straw, and not with newspaper as is the custom.
And he lay at home in his father's hut for his wake. And the
children from the neighbourhood sang over his still green face.
And his eyes were propped open with thorns so that he might
see his god when he entered heaven, because, they said, children
were innocent. And there was no weeping either at the wake
or the funeral. Even Antonio held back his tears, because they
all agreed that children were well out of this life, and what hope
could there ever be for a green boy?

Dr Bertoloni and the Soft Fruits

There was a place on the hacienda where blue birds used to perch in wild orange trees high above a rift of watery ferns. They called it The Zanjón. Really it was just one of many, and yet, somehow, so cool and still with nothing to stir the air but blue wings settling that it earned its title. Then there was a ridge halfway up the hill behind the Big House where a bamboo plant had towered and colonized the sloping field, spreading some forty feet into the sky. It was a clump of wedded canes that invaded a whole field with its girth and shade. The foreman's four cows used to graze there, privileged on those hot days to chew their cud under its spidery leaves. Then, after the sugar cane was cut, there was running across the padded field of strewn leaves, yellowing in the sun and still prickly. It calmed me to run across what had so recently been a living barrier into a new horizon; even though it was just the same horizon of the year before and the year before that when the cane was harvested and the land laid bare. These were the things that eased my restlessness; these, and Dr Bertoloni, the wandering vet who arrived at that remote hacienda in a remote part of the Andes once or twice a year. He would always turn up unannounced, materializing in the courtyard with his canvas bag of tools and drugs and saws and, despite our uncanny closeness, he would always leave in tears.

Dr Bertoloni was a nomad. He had no home, and not even a country to claim as his own. He had left Italy as a mere boy and never returned after forty years of wandering. On his arrival there was a ritual that was always kept to. So, first, he would drink a glass of cold water under the avocado tree that stood guard over the Big House. Then I would offer coffee, which he would refuse.

The house was open on three sides with a procession of pillars leading back into the various rooms. Inside, blocking the middle of three tall arches, was a long carved bench. It came, originally, from the Cathedral of Trujillo, and I never knew how or why exactly it came to rest its eighteen feet of worn seat and elaborately carved back in the Big House. It was on this bench that we would sit and discuss the state of my sheep and dogs and cows, and it was on the same bench that we would eventually discuss the soft fruits.

Whenever an animal died on the hacienda, whether it was mine or one of the workers', the body would be kept 'in case Dr Bertoloni came by'. These dead specimens were always kept for him for a day or two, but the climate was sub-tropical and after forty-eight hours the already sick flesh would be so decayed that instead of a burial there would be a cremation. The sweet sickly smell of bad meat burning would fill the air for hours. Hours of remembering his stone-grey eyes that deepened into blue, the rare flash of his smile and the sadness of his hands. Dr Bertoloni had beautiful hands, like a pianist; but his fingers had long since been transposed to cure the sick, and draw the knowledge of hindsight only out of dead organs. There were many animals on the hacienda, and many more diseases, so as often as not there would be a corpse, large or small, waiting for him to inspect and dissect when his jeep ground up the stony drive.

The animals were inspected in strict order, starting with the dogs, and then again the pack of imported beagles had precedence over the Siberian husky, the mad Dalmatian and Winston, a lugubrious and ancient basset-hound who suffered from a supposedly lethal condition called sarcoma. The years passed over this old hound's head, and his disease, which took the form of cancerous sores on his already unnaturally large penis, seemed of more interest to the vet and me than to him. After the dogs, it was the turn of cows and sheep, chickens and ducks and then whatever else was lurking around the house, ranging from monkeys to tame vultures, eaglets and wolverines.

Only after all the animals had been seen and the last of the clamouring children from the hills had returned with their bundles of wriggling pigs or rabbits under their arms, and the autopsy, if there was to be one, had been done, would Dr Bertoloni come into the house and sit down. Matilde, the cook, would serve him coffee, shuffling painfully towards the carved bench. Together with his miniature cup, she would give him a fleeting glance of the sympathy she had for this stranger who had surgically divided his life into so much for one farmstead, and so much for the next, leaving nothing in reserve for himself. Matilde always brewed the sugar in with the coffee over the stove, and the pinch of scorn that she also felt for the visiting vet was as well mixed with her tenderness as the sweetness in the proffered drink. To care about animals was all to the good. Had she not bottle-fed a lamb and given it her old aprons to chew? But to not care for money at all was a sin. And then, if she limped and lurched as she stumbled through her work it was because a wild cow had charged her. You never knew quite what to make of a man who'd stick his arm, to the elbow, up a cow's backside. Kindness or no, she'd soak his cup in soda after he left, like she always did, because . . . you never knew, and cows were trouble; and so much heat – mercy, didn't anyone else feel it?

Matilde would retreat, muttering under her breath as she always did, concocting recipes for her aches and pains as her days passed in a cycle of coffee dregs and stews.

On his first visit Dr Bertoloni had established himself as an Italian, a fellow European, a travelled man who had been forty years in Venezuela and was homeless here now by choice rather than necessity. For me, in that place that had few visitors, he was a welcome change from the gruellingly simple routine of the hacienda. And, since there were no other Europeans, he was the one link with my past, a lever to the battened holds of my language and family and memories of things grown alien in their exile. So I tried constantly to draw him out on this, our common front, but Dr Bertoloni would not or could not talk about Italy or even France or Spain. Our talks would be of other things, of syndromes in the sheep and dogs, of remedies for bloat, of milk and paraffin to block the fermentation in a grassy gut, of ways to keep my harpy-eaglet well, of how the sugar cane was flowering high, all punctuated by silence. Our mutual shyness could fill an afternoon with this, the silence of unspoken desires, a need to cling, a search for straws, and the continual sense of treading water in the hot sickly sea of the tropics.

Whatever yearnings he had in his life, whatever hopes or aims, I never knew, nor could I spell out my own predicament, my sense of imprisonment. I cannot to this day define what it is or was that I felt for Dr Bertoloni, I only know that I lived from season to season waiting for the sound of his battered jeep.

Like the woodworm and the giant bees that bored into the fabric of the Big House, I kept digging at my visitor's past. I had discovered that he was unmarried and unattached, homeless and landless and happy to remain that way. Each piece of information became like a contour on the map of him that I was drawing in my mind. It was as though I couldn't see him if I couldn't see what lay behind him. I felt that I would lose precious moments of communion if I did not hold the clues to all his ways inside my head. I never learnt his name. He said it hurt to hear it spoken, even by himself, so he remained Dr Bertoloni through all our meetings.

Once, when he arrived and the sheep had anthrax, he stayed for several days and we worked together enclosing the roofed but otherwise open stables to gather the infected sheep in and fight, day and night, to save the flock.

My sheep had travelled round the world, further than either of us. Four hundred Romney Marshes shipped from Australia so slowly that when they arrived whoever had originally ordered them had grown bored and no longer wanted his living consignment. They were brought to me in lorries, across the Orinocan plains where an anonymous donor had added the dubious gift of two hundred Afrikaner sheep from the South African veld. These last were like red deer, short-haired, bony and restless. Crammed into the cattle trucks they had kicked and bucked their tired woollen hosts, trampling the weaker ones on to the floor of the wagon. A quarter of the flock were scraped out dead on arrival, the rest were nursed back to health and put to graze on the many slopes and valleys of the hacienda. The peasant workers had never seen sheep before and they disbelieved the tales they heard of their wool and meat. Goats were goats and where they ate nothing grew again. Each jawful of scrub cost a piece of land and land was everything. Goats gave you milk and one or two were all right, but their hooves beat out a strange tom-tom on the hills. People spoke of the state of Lara, where goats had turned the land into a desert, and only cacti and poverty grew.

When the lorries arrived, a circle of curious peasants stood round and watched the unloading of the carcasses and walking wounded. Meat was something that was eaten at Christmas when the annual pig was killed, or sometimes there was a chicken from their yards; they liked meat, but they didn't like the look of this sort, hobbling manured and urinated on to their fold. It would take a long time to persuade the peasants that the thousands of empty hectares could successfully rear sheep and feed them all. It was an experiment, a challenge that I shared with Dr Bertoloni. Together we would change the face of the Andes with these unlikely sheep. But the sheep themselves didn't know it. Sometimes they seemed to need a psychiatrist more than a vet, it was as though the long voyage had sapped their will to live. Then the first lambs came. Some of the boys from the hacienda even volunteered at this stage to work with them and me. A new ram came, sent down from the dizzying heights of the Páramo, and with it came anthrax to the pen by the house

I had spent over a year with these sheep. The treating and the killing and the cremating that ensued sickened me. Every time I closed my eyes I seemed to hear the sound of crushed glass under the skin, the crackling edema of anthrax in my ears.

As for Dr Bertoloni, he abandoned the usual detached approach to his patients, and threw himself into their salvation as though his own life depended on their cure. While we worked, he told me that he had grown up a shepherd, sleeping out with his family's flock of milk ewes in Liguria in Northern Italy from the age of eight. He told me of the days spent dreaming against trees and stones while he watched his flock. Sometimes three or four days would go by without his seeing any other human being.

'It used to scare me,' he said, in his edged Spanish, 'to talk to myself, but the silence of the hills seemed to move towards me and I had to make it move back, so I used to talk to the sheep. They never stayed very long to listen, so I began to talk to leaves and stones. I scarcely knew my family. My brothers all worked, my sister was ill, my mother had no time for me – it was all used up trying to make ends meet – and my father had that harshness of a man who has failed but will not admit it. It was the times that were hard, and there were too many of us.

'I lived with the sheep for three years, and the flock dwindled, not through any neglect of mine, but because it had to be eaten or sold to fill the pot. Gradually everything had to go, our stone house which had never had much in it was stripped bare.

'My sister died. I don't remember it though. One week I went up into the hills and she was lying where she always did on a mat against the kitchen wall, and the next week she was gone. Everything went in the end. Even me. When I was eleven my father walked me for two days into Reggio nell Emilia, and I shepherded another flock there for my keep and whatever sum was paid over on my arrival. It seemed fair. My new sheep were plump and the pasture was good. I slept in my master's stable-loft with the other men and boys who worked for him, and we ate well.

'I learnt to read out in the fields. I knew more kindness at my patron's farm than I had ever known before. For a month or so I was aware of his watching me while I worked. He would stand some hundred yards away and stare past me. The older hands said that I looked a little like his own son lost in the war, and I thought that maybe by staring at me he could see his boy beyond. I was careful when he came not to slacken at my work. But when he left me to myself, and later when the summer came, I used to read while half-watching his flock, or roam the fields gathering the soft fruits from the hedgerows and eating them. They were the same soft fruits of my babyhood, the cherries and berries and grapes that seemed to spring up from nowhere. All that summer I was drunk with my happiness, and then . . . I was caught reading at my work, and summoned to il padrone.

'I didn't fear the beating, I'd grown up with a father who thought it a sign of weakness to unclench his fist. I went, determined to plead with him. I'd beg and offer all I had: my time and meagre strength, if he would only keep me on.'

All through this tale we had been performing the perfunctory duties of doctor and nurse, straddling one sheep after another and injecting them. We reached the end of the batch just as Dr Bertoloni reached this point in his story, and he just stopped, then strode off down the drive to collect something. I waited in the dim light of the stable with the acrid greasy smell of the sheep floating out into the night. Ten minutes went by and he still did not return. He was standing now beside his jeep, staring up into the misty stars. I called to him, but he was so lost in thought that he didn't even turn. I gathered my syringes together and went back into the Big House to get a drink and sit on the bench with the heavy scent of the night jasmine slowly drowning the sick smell of the sheep with its successive waves of fragrance.

It was some time later when Dr Bertoloni joined me there. The servants and all the household had gone to bed at either end of the house, leaving the entire middle section with its cavernous arches to ourselves and the heavy jasmine. He came and slumped down wearily on the bench, which was our bench because it was always here that we sat and reminisced of the soft fruits of Europe. He picked up his story as abruptly as he had stopped.

'He kept me like a son from then on. I went to school and lived in his house. I was twelve, and he and his wife seemed to have infinite patience with me. I had to learn at school, and I had to learn in their house about beds and plumbing and forks and collars. It was a strange, strange time. My religion was his gentleness and my ambition to please him. I know that I was his surrogate son. He sent me to university in Perugia, and when Mussolini and the blackshirts began to show signs of war he sent me to Paris, to the Sorbonne, to study there and be away from any chance of violence. He hated it so much. He used to say, 'Why shouldn't I hate it, whatever the cause? It took my son away, I won't let it take his shadow.'

'When the War did come, it took him. I only went back once. His farm was destroyed, his house flattened, the fields pitted with shrapnel and scrap. There was no trace of him or of his wife or of any of his farmhands. I had French papers in those days, I had been given them by him and then kept them for years. Pasteur, that was the name he gave me, and that's right in a way. I am a shepherd. I always was.

'I've never been back to Italy again. I don't know if I have any family. When I looked that one time they too had gone and all that was left were some crumbling stones where we once used to live. No bombs had fallen on their home. Something drove them out . . . probably the same poverty that always did. And I've never been back to France, or to Spain where I herded sheep after I got my degree, trying to return to the simplicity of existing alone. Sometimes I can hardly remember what those countries are like. The only things I never forget are the soft fruits . . .'

His eyes had the transparent blueness of the Ligurian Sea, looking into them I felt a strange mixture of contentment and sadness. Maybe he would never tell any more about himself, and yet the casting of names that he so often did, his conjuring up of the most obscure soft fruits in the woods, was like an unravelling of himself. I began to think that with his lists of names he was in fact telling me both his past and my future.

He worried about my isolation on the hacienda. He would constantly ask me, 'Aren't you lonely?' and I would lie that I wasn't. But it was no good lying to him because the depth of his clear eyes could swallow you under and throw you back to the surface knowing you in ways that you did not know yourself. So he'd always say, 'You can't be alone after you have known people and love and life. You can't. It's just pretending. Loneliness is born of itself, once there has been contact you are a part of life whether you like it or not, you can go with or against the tide or you can drown.' So he worried about me, and I worried about him, and together we remembered the peaches and apricots, strawberries and plums of our youth: two youths with half a century between them, joined in a memory of gooseberries and grapes.

The first fruits were easy to recall, it was the later ones, the ones that formed the last half of our litany, that cost great feats of memory, dredging up half-forgotten names in English, Spanish, French and Italian while savouring their tastes vicariously down the years. It excited a pleasure that was at once sensual and almost sacred. He would gaze across the trellised flowers and then exclaim,

'Greengages!'

Then we would pause to remember the bluish hue on the skin, the smell of the fruit warmed in the sun, the first twist of taste.

'Bilberries.'

If, on preceding visits, a particular fruit had not been named at all, it would score an impact that left him lost in admiration for a few seconds.

'And loganberries.'

'Cherries.'

'Morello Cherries.'

'Raspberries.'

'Redcurrants.'

'Blackcurrants.'

'Whitecurrants that hide under the weeds.'

'Wild strawberries.'

'Crab apples.'

'Damsons.'

'Sloes.'

Each name dragged back a memory and each memory was locked in a sad compartment of his eyes. Each name brought back a moment of my childhood to that place where I had been forced to grow prematurely old. They bit into our nostalgia with the bitter-sweet tang of wild fruit. The Andes mountains and the Atlantic Ocean stood between us and them. The soothing familiarity of those names always brought tears to the painfully gentle blue of his gaze. He would often joke about his homelessness and how little it bothered him to be constantly on the move, but the ritual of the soft fruits dragged out splinters of the bombed and abandoned homes that he had once known. All that he knew was scattered and gone except for these memories of fruit gathered on his own and culled now on the hem of the wild hills that harboured so many alien fruits of their own.

The Siren

When I was a child, I lived by the sea, in a pink terraced house on the edge of Porthmeor beach. From my bedroom window I could see the lifeboat being towed in and out of the water to the fishing boats in winter, and I could see the red flag for dangerous bathing, waving like a red rag to the local boys. I knew all the contours of our beach; the space between each breakwater, and the times of the tides and the best places to find the fattest bladder-wrack. After each storm, the beach would be littered with driftwood and jetsam and sea-glass and hundreds of new shells.

I used to collect shells and hide them in an old hatbox in the attic. My mother didn't let me keep shells or other things from the sea in our house. Our front room looked down the beach and out across the Cornish coast, but mother rarely used it. She preferred the kitchen at the back where she was in control. The front room had too many keys in it, too many sour memories. My father was a sailor, and the sea kept taking him away. The last time he left, I was eight years old, and he still hasn't kept his promise to come home, but he will. He often went away before that, but every few months or so, and once for a year, he used to come back, laden with presents that he said came from China, but that mother said came from a shop she knew in Charlestown.

She used to say that he'd never come back. Sometimes she even told her own mother that he was a no good runaway. But I knew that it was the sea that kept him, and the sea itself would bring him home, so I kept scanning the horizon and watching the tides and combing the sands for signs, and waiting. I wasn't allowed to ask when he'd be home, it was bad for mother's

nerves, and mother suffered from her nerves. She carried a
little glass bottle around with her which she sniffed from time
to time, and when she wasn't smelling it, she seemed to sniff
just the same, as though she missed whatever was kept inside.
She told me it contained smelling salts, and I felt better, because
I knew that although she pretended not to, she really did
love my daddy too. To this day, when I smell the salt tang
of the Atlantic it reminds me of him; and it comforted me
to think that mother carried her own bottled nostalgia around
with her, together with her high blood pressure and her
nerves.

My mother was a tall thin woman, with lines on her face and
hands that creased into a mask and gloves of worry at the
slightest provocation. Since we lived on our own, it was usually
I who provoked her. Our next door neighbour was a baker, and
she kept a little shop in her house, selling pasties and bread and
lardy cakes. She was always very nice to me. I asked her once
why mother had so many creases on her face, and she said that
it was all that my father had left her. I felt sorry after that,
because all my daddy gave to her was worry, while he had given
me the sound of the sea.

Every time daddy came home, I was sent out to sit on the
step or walk on the beach while mother reminded him of
all that he had forgotten and told him how hard her life was
and how her heart was hardening. Daddy wasn't allowed to
speak. Whatever he said, she just shouted, 'I don't believe
you.'

Sometimes she used to do that with me. While my parents
were having what the baker called one of their 'reconciliations',
they would both completely forget about me. Our neighbour
used to bring me things to eat while I waited, or take me in to
hers; and to reassure me she would say, 'He'll win her round,
Mary, don't you worry, he always does. Your father may not
be much of a sailor, but he can always navigate his way through
a skirt, you'll see, they'll be calling you in for tea before you
know it.'

We would use granny's old Doulton teapot and there would be
a heap of cinnamon toast. Mother would drink her tea, red-eyed

and with her upper lip trembling slightly on the cup. Whenever my father was away, she responded to her loneliness by pursing her mouth very tightly, as though she kept the housekeeping in there and was afraid that it would fall out. The only times that she would smile would be if daddy stayed for more than a week. In between, she would let her face relax and her mouth would tremble as it decided, slowly, whether it was safe to smile.

The best time of my life would come when, hand in hand, daddy and I would climb down the stone steps to the beach. He had big smooth hands with black hairs on the backs of his fingers and a gold ring below the biggest of his knuckles, made of gold from the Guinea coast. He had a tattoo on one forearm with a heart and my name, 'Mary', written in it which he said was for me so that he would never forget me when he went away to sea. Mother was a bit jealous of that tattoo and tried to pretend that it had been there even before I was born, but she liked his other one, with the green eagle eating a snake which a Red Indian had done. My father was as dark as a pirate chief and he had black curly hair that used to fall into his eyes, and a black moustache that he used to chew when he felt restless. I was dark too, shaped from his rib like sculpted driftwood and dyed with ship's tar, he said. I was glad not to be blonde and wrinkled like my mother, although I really did love her too. I just couldn't help loving my father better.

He loved the beach. It was he who had chosen our house, near enough to the sea to hear its waves crashing and to watch its whispering spume drag along the sand. We used to walk for hours with our shoes in our hands or tied and strung round our necks. He'd pick up the little shells and tell me what they were, and I'd listen as though I didn't know. Porthmeor was rich in limpets and mussels, razor shells and the white corally cuttles. But the shell shops in the village sold other kinds of shells, polished and gleaming with their exotic colours. Daddy used to buy me abalone and mother-of-pearl.

He'd take the big shells and hold them to his ear and smile.

'That's the sweetest sound in the whole world, Mary, the sound of the sea.'

Then he'd pass it to me so that I could listen too, and out of the hollowness I could really hear the waves tumbling in a far distance.

'If you were a boy, I'd take you away to sail on the oceans; but the sea is not for girls, Mary.'

Talking by the sea used to make daddy strangely pensive, he'd jump from one subject to another, stirring the pool of his thoughts as though with a shrimping net, pulling out now a starfish, now an anemone and sometimes just a handful of grit.

'Men aren't so bad, you know, despite what your mother tells you. I'm not such a bad chap either. Sailors never could settle down. Some people were made to roam. I wish I could stay with you, just the two of us . . . I never could stand nagging . . . your mother was so different when I first knew her.'

At night, when I was supposed to be asleep, I heard the muttered grumbling from my parents' bedroom, and I could tell, from the occasional sound of mother's weeping, that daddy would be leaving again soon. Their hushed sounds of disagreement were as clear to me as a ship's siren drifting through the night. My father would pack his kitbag and go again, and my mother would purse her lips and drag back her hair once more, and fall prey to her nerves and I would be left with my memories and the attic and my shells and the beach, until he came back for me.

He always came back, year after year, until I was eight and I grew ill and lost his sound and the sea swallowed him up for always. I thought that he was drowned, but mother just said that she wished he was but he couldn't be. She refused to talk about him any more, and I had to learn to live without him. None of the other children seemed to understand what it was like to have lost a sailor, except for Susan and Emily Pawson whose father's fishing boat had capsized off Lands End and he had drowned before the lifeboat found him. But their mother talked about him, and took them to his graveside in the cemetery to remember him, and there was a photograph of Mr Pawson

on their mantelpiece looking out from under his sou'-wester.
So I played a bit with Susan, but Emily was mean, and she
didn't like me.

Mother thought playing was a waste of time, but I had so
much time on my hands I didn't know what to do with it. She
suggested sewing, but it didn't suit me. I preferred to climb
through the trap-door into the attic and pretend that I had a
boat of my own with a mast and sail and oars to row it with,
and to sit by the tiny dormer-window watching the waves with
daddy's shell close to my ear, listening. I knew, whatever
anyone said, that if he wasn't drowned my father would come
back to me. Even when I was twelve and thirteen and older, I
could still remember his face and his voice, I could remember
him saying, 'When you have a man, Mary, bear with him a
bit, and be kind to him. Kindness goes a long way. Not weak,
you understand, but not sour. The sea is salt, but it's never
sour.'

I used to dream that when I fell in love, my man would be
just like him, and I'd be so kind that he'd never go away and
not come back. And he'd be dark like me and my daddy, and
none of his nerves would be out on the surface or strung so
tightly inside him that they would snap. For his tea I would
make him mountains of cinnamon toast. So long as he loved
me, I would never reproach him or make him remember the
things that he wanted to forget. He'd be a sailor. After each
voyage he would bring me presents from the West Indies or
the South Seas; our front room would be full of fans and shawls
and carved wooden things without a single dust cover stitched
over them. I'd never tell our children he was a ne'er-do-well.
And if he drowned I'd never say that it was in sin with a fat
woman in Charlestown. But he wouldn't be lost at sea, anyway,
he'd always be sailing home.

When I was seventeen we moved to Charlestown and I took a
job in the yachting shop, working at the till. I had heard a lot
of rumours about my father, and not just the bitter stories that
my mother told. It seemed that I might find him there, so I
began to look for him. I drank in the pubs along the harbour,
listening to the fishermen and sailors talk, hoping that I would

hear his name or find a friend who would lead me to him. Mother called me a slut when she discovered that I went into bars on my own, but I didn't mind. We weren't getting along at all well by then.

One evening, I think it was October, I saw my father sitting in a corner with his back to me, but by the time I had prepared how best to show myself, and gone to greet him, he wasn't there any more. Another time, I saw him walk past the shop. I left the till and ran out after him. I wanted to call 'daddy' but my voice had shrivelled up. So I caught up with him, instead, and held him by the shoulder until he turned around.

That was how I met Spiros, the image of my father, and the man who loved me more than all the world, more than his own island, he said. He came from the island of Antipaxos, and I was the kindness that he found in a foreign land. They called him Spiros the Greek on the quay. But he spoke English with the same sweet west-country lilt as my father. He didn't need to tell me that he was a sailor, I could tell by the way he walked and by the wonderful restlessness in his flecked brown eyes. His body moved to the rhythm of the tides, and, morning and evening, waves of his own self washed over me.

Mother hated him from the start. She said that he was too like my father to be true, and that his hands were too soft to be a sailor's and his head was full of lies. I would have loved him anyway, but I loved him more after mother died. He moved into the little house she left me and I spoilt him in every way I could, trying not to think of the haemorrhage in my mother's brain that had killed her in the High Street. He told me that we would be married when he came back from his next voyage, and he gave me a ring and left me a lace petticoat to remember him by.

He said that he might be away for as long as two months, but I didn't mind. I've waited two years now, but I know he'll come home, he promised me. I spent the first winter downstairs, making double cinnamon toast in case he came home and was cold and hungry. I had a job then as a waitress in the Two White Cocks, but I gave it up because the sailors there kept telling me that Spiros wasn't one of them at all. They said he wasn't even Greek in anything except the darkness of his curls. But he was my man, and I bore with him, just as I always will.

The lady from the Social Services says that I should get out of the house and fill in forms. There is time enough for that, though, when Spiros comes home. She keeps complaining about the coldness here, being on the edge of town, now that the gas is disconnected, but I'm not cold at all. I feel hot inside. I wish the window looked out towards the sea, but it doesn't matter, because I can always hear it. I like it best when it snows, and the grass in the park billows.

Sometimes I think that mother understood more than I did. I wanted my two men to live in ships. Or I thought I did. But really I want them here, with me. Daddy said that girls could never sail. Perhaps he wanted me to understand that some people are sailors in their dreams. I shouldn't have kept asking for such exotic fans. I shouldn't have kept pushing them. When they come back, both, or either of them, I'll never do that again. I've got my own things now, the old ones that I had as a child, and I can circumnavigate the world from here. That's why I stay in the attic, so that they'll know I'm bearing with them.

After the funeral, I went through mother's things and found some photographs of my father. I showed them to Spiros, I'd already told him how much I missed the only other sailor that I'd known. Spiros missed him too, after that, he was never quite the same. He grew so restless that I didn't know how to please him any more. He asked me a lot of questions about my daddy, and I loved him more for that; I'd never known anyone so interested in him. Then, one day, he packed his kitbag and he told me that he had to go. He was angry with his own father, he had been since I started talking about mine.

The lady from the Social Services says Spiros will never come home. But I don't believe her. I don't open the door to her any more, not to anyone. They don't understand how busy I am, waiting. They even tried to take me away, but I won't go. I'm quite safe here, and I don't feel the cold. It's only sourness that kills, and the sea. There's nothing here to pick my bones; and the shell sound is waiting with me. I shan't remind Spiros of the years or of Antipaxos or any Greek islands when he comes home. I'll just make his cinnamon toast, and smile, and show that I know how to bear with a man.

Garter

For anyone passing along the uneven band of greyness that was the road between the South London Hospital for Women and the Clock Tower, the Common had a dour flat look with its alternate stretches of balding mud and windswept sweet papers. At best, it was a place to gather conkers, at worst, a short cut to run across, a place of menace whose edges held a frayed threat of their own.

Once a year a circus came, towing its marquees and trailers and camels and candy floss; and then the funfair with its young men in black leather who carried silvery chains and whose hair seemed to grow the wrong way in black spikes, and who tipped Fanta tins into the boating pond. We were never allowed to visit the circus, but we watched the preparations from the edge of the Common. We had also been warned never to so much as look at these young men in black leather, but we did.

After the funfairs and the circus had left, my sister and I used to cover the ground where they had been, discovering a hint of the thrill of the big top in the massive droppings and the fallen cartridge-cases. Once, we had even bought pass tickets into the circus ground, although we had no money for any of the side-shows, or for the big top itself. One of the side-shows had been a bearded lady, but we had already seen one of those on the 118 bus that stopped at the Old Town. Another of the side-shows was a fat lady, but she didn't seem at all unusual to us, it was the Siamese twins, 'born today', that we were most sorry to have missed.

It was after the departure of one of these funfairs that I first met Garter. I had noticed him once or twice on my way to school, sweeping by the plague pond in the middle of the lower hem of the Common. I had a fear of road-sweepers in general, a kind of social embarrassment and revulsion rolled into one. So, from the first time I had noticed him, I watched out from my coveted front seat on the upstairs of a number 118, with a sense of fascination. He was always there with his heavy-headed street-broom and his bottle-end glasses tied together with wire and string. He always wore the same threadbare grey suit. He didn't really move like other people, he was very slow.

I had pointed him out once to my mother, from the downstairs of the bus. She didn't like the smoke, and what she called the yobbos on the top, and I used to pretend that I didn't either when I was with her, but I did. She looked at my road-sweeper, almost through her nostrils, in a way she had, and she said that she wouldn't like to meet *him* on a dark night. This gave him a further air of mystery, and in the winter evenings, when his work had come full circle, and he was back by the plague pond,. silhouetted against the willow on its island in the middle by the streetlights, I felt an urge to speak to my road-sweeper, and once, when I was on the inside of the aisle, and he couldn't see, I waved.

Later, I asked my mother to explain what she meant about him and the dark night, but I could get nothing from her, except that 'he was not the kind of man to be trusted with furry animals'. I had never known such a person, and when he spoke to me, from his avenue of sodden leaves beside the littered fair site, I was quick to reply. From then on, we spoke regularly, and I began to walk across the edge of the Common twice a day. He noticed all the days when I didn't come, and he took as keen an interest in the ups and downs of my tubercular glands as any of my doctors. He told me that his name was Garter, and whenever I asked him about his work or himself, he would always say, 'I'm doing all right,' then he would wait for what seemed like an uncomfortably long time, and finally add, 'but I would like you to do better.'

I was always very touched by this man's concern to keep me from sweeping the gutter as he did. He worried about the illness in my glands, and I worried about his stammer and the way he dribbled when he spoke.

At Christmas I gave him a pound note, but he gave it back to me, saying, 'I d-don't want money, I want l-l-love.'

I was very hurt, and went home and gave the money to my sister. I didn't know how anyone could love Garter, with his grey suit thinned in the wind behind, and starched with years of OK sauce and egg down the front, and his lank greasy hair plastered down with the flakes of what I took to be a scalp infection.

On the days when my fever rose I didn't go out at all, and so I didn't get to see him, but I still thought about him, his refusal of my money, and, considering his appearance, what I thought to be his unreasonable demand for love. I tried to imagine him as the furry animal that my mother thought he could not be trusted with. As I lay in bed (and I was allowed to lie in my mother's double bed whenever I was ill, and use the wireless during the day, and borrow all my sister's pillows) I would close my eyes between the cramps in my side, and manage to imagine Garter as a kind of aging mole with a matted grey coat of fur, balding and caked in places like his suit, his tiny eyes strained away from both sunlight and lamps as though in pain, and his fingernails full of earth and compacted grime – it just seemed possible. I thought, someone could love him, but although he could move me, more perhaps than anyone else at the time, it couldn't be me. I wondered if he had a mother. Even Garter had to have a mother, and I set out to tell him this one morning, truanting from my sick-bed to do so.

He had worked his way along the slabs and gutters to the small lake, no bigger than a large concrete pond, where middle-aged men and children went at weekends to race their model boats. The walk had made me dizzy, and when I found him, Garter put his hand out to hold my arm. I shrank back from his touch, and then I was embarrassed. In those days, I shrank back from everybody's touch, I had a kind of neurasthaenia of the skin, but he couldn't have known that.

'You must have a mother, Garter,' I told him.

'Course I have, Missus,' he said. He always called me Missus when I was alone with him.

'Well,' I said, 'she must love you.'

But Garter surprised me with his matter-of-fact reply.

'No, she never loved me, Missus, said I was soft.'

I was sorry to have introduced such an unsuccessful topic, and I tried to make amends.

'She probably did love you a little bit,' I said.

'No, Missus,' he said, and paused, the way he often did, with finality, but somehow always in mid-sentence. Then, after several minutes while we both shuffled uneasily on the pavement, Garter brightened, and said, 'But she did make me cakes.'

That was the one moment of perfect ease in our friendship. I didn't love this strange slow man either, but I, too, could make him cakes.

That night I made a batch of chocolate buns from Fanny Farmer's Boston Cookbook. It was the recipe that we always used, and the page itself was so caked with the ingredients that one could see at a glance all that was needed. Next morning I took the cakes to Garter. I had decided to miss school, and I took the long way across the Common.

This began on the corner of the 'SS murder', opposite the first entrance to the old war bunker that rose like a beached whale out of the grass, flanked by a pair of public lavatories that, like so many other things in that wasted area, we were not allowed to use. Then, still following the edge, up towards Wandsworth, where we never went, I walked along the avenue of peeling plane-trees, past the scarred part where the circus came and squatted once a year. Then the walk turned in to the stunted may trees and the path to the swings and then, on the far side, the bandstand where boys on roller-skates tried to knock you down. As I neared the swings, I turned again, we were in trouble with the lady who doled out the drinking-water and broke up fights. Before I was even halfway across the indistinct football pitch, I could see Garter on the far side of the pond, sweeping in slow-motion as he always did.

In retrospect, I believe that our friendship changed from the day of the cakes. Garter began to confide in me, with what I now found an alarming insistence. The pauses between any word of his and the next could be so long that all meaning would be lost, but gradually I began to sense his drift. I was divided between my fear of his slowness, and my fear of hurting his feelings by letting our friendship drop.

Once, I remember, he asked me to put my hand in his pocket. He was smiling a strange leering smile such as I imagined him to have when he became the furry mole who had seen better times. I hesitated then, at least as long as he himself did. I considered everything. I considered running away, shouting for help, even drowning in the round pond that already held so many ancient corpses locked in its mud. Finally, I said, 'No.'

But Garter was ready for me, barring the pavement with his long broom-handle.

'Go on, Missus,' he said.

Again I waited, and then I put my gloved hand in his pocket with such loathing that I felt physically sick. I don't know what I expected to find, a dead newt, a slice of raw liver, a stag-beetle. But, from the seat of my dread, the last thing I expected to find was a bag of chocolate buttons.

'They're for you,' Garter stammered, 'I buyed them.'

Despite my relief, I didn't see Garter again for over a week. It was my longest absence yet. I had left the chocolate buttons and my gloves on the top of a bus, on purpose, but the gloves had been handed in at school, and my name-tabs brought them back to me. At least the sweets were gone. I threw the gloves at the railway lines that ran under the bridge from the gardens to the playing-fields, and it pleased me that they fell on to an oncoming train.

At last, I relented, and returned to our rendezvous, but Garter had gone. There was a new road-sweeper, and I was surprised to see that, by comparison, he seemed quite normal. After another week, I asked him where Garter was.

'They've moved him on again,' he said bluntly, and turned back to his work.

'Oh,' I said, turning to go as well, 'so he hasn't had an accident or anything?'

'Not yet,' his replacement told me, with a touch of un-pleasantness in his voice. 'But you never know when a soft one like that will start molesting.'

'What do you mean?' I asked.

'Little girls,' he laughed, 'little girls like you.'

I couldn't resist asking him, 'What does he do to them?' But I could see that Garter's replacement was irked by my presence.

'How the Hell should I know, but there's been a complaint. Now clear off, will you?'

Garter had told me earlier that he never spoke to anyone but me from one day to the next, and I was shocked to think that he had lost his place by the plague pond because of me. I began to read my mother's newspaper after her, scanning the columns for news of molesting, and asking questions, but I could find out nothing more specific about molesting, although I knew that it wasn't anything to do with moles, even if Garter sometimes did look a bit like one. It was always the same, I wanted to know what they did. I knew what a murderer was, we discussed the likes of them in the playground, but this new character, this so-called child-molester seemed to have no place in the spoken world around me. If it was a crime to touch me, then all the people who had held my face and kissed my head and rumpled my hair and who all without exception made me squirm, surely they should be 'moved on' first. However, there was something about Garter that made me feel ill. I decided that far from I being his victim, he was mine. During that time when I didn't see him, even the smell of a thousand spilt dinners that he carried around with him faded into the rich leafy smell of the Common.

It was just after my twelfth birthday that I found him again. I had become, once more, an out-patient at the South London Hospital which looked out over the bunker and the lavatories at the edge of the Common. I went in every day, before school, for an injection. One day, Garter was standing, leaning with his stubbly chin on his broom-handle outside the railings of the ambulance ramp. I couldn't decide what to do, whether to go back into the hospital and leave through another entrance, to ignore him or to say hello. But it was he who saw me first, miraculously through the dim lenses of his glasses. He was less than a mile away from where he had been before. He told me that he had nearly died, earlier, when they moved him down to Tooting, to the edge of the Common there. Garter seemed quite overcome, and I made him walk along the street in the hopes that no one would notice the rivulets of tears that were coming from under his glasses. After a while, I said, 'I have to go now, Garter, I'll see you again soon.'

He looked suddenly startled, as though remembering something that hurt.

'They moved me because of you, you know, Missus,' he said sadly, and then he paused. Two 118s came round the corner of Cavendish Road and up to the edge of the Common while I waited for Garter to speak again. He looked as though he might actually burst, such was his effort to overcome this phase of his silent stammer, suddenly he said, 'I need you, you're the only friend I've ever had. You never laugh at me, and you gave me some cakes and I buyed you some chocolate.'

This was the longest speech that he had ever made to me, and I squeezed his arm of my own accord, and wished that I had eaten those sweets, and ran away to catch my bus, laden with guilt.

After that, I spoke to him every day on my way to and from the hospital. I took upon myself the responsibility of keeping our meetings very brief, and of avoiding seeing him after dark. Every morning when I saw him, tears would gather and curl round the edges of his spectacles, and he would say, as regularly now as he had once said good morning, 'I thought you wasn't coming.'

I continued to see him daily for another six months. Sometimes, days in my mother's bed would keep me away. At other times, it would be hard to leave him crying in the street when I said I had to catch my bus again. But gradually he seemed to settle down into his new rhythm of sweeping leaves and salting sludge and gathering up the endless sweet papers and the cigarette-ends. It seemed that Garter and I had found a way to live together.

I was questioned about Garter in May. I had feared that such a thing might happen the previous December, when we were reunited, and Garter used to walk beside me weeping, but by May he had stopped doing that. He was just a quiet elderly man with a worn grey suit and dirty hair. A harmless, motherless man who spent his days sweeping in slow-motion to suit his slow brain. But the officer who questioned me didn't think so. He asked me twice, 'Has he touched you?' And I lied for him, 'No.' Then he said, 'But he does talk to you. We've seen him.'

I nodded.

'What does he say?' he asked, kindlier now.

'Nothing,' I said, 'he doesn't say anything.'

'Well, he must say something,' he smiled.

'He just says he needs me,' I said, 'nothing else.'

'Well, that's all right then, isn't it,' the officer said, and I went home.

Next morning, Garter had gone. I looked for signs of him on the edge of the Common, both by the round pond and the bunker, and I even went down to Tooting on my bicycle and rode all day along the tree-lined streets. But I never found him again. All that year I walked on the Common, watching the horse chestnut leaves unfurling and falling, but the conkers and the funfair and the swings and even the bandstand lost their hold on me. Even the autumn leaves seemed dull, and it always seemed to be autumn. In November, the fevers returned, and I spent another year engrossed in my tubercular glands, and it was these that enabled me to stop searching for Garter with his grey suit and his stammer and his glasses tied together with wire and string, Garter who said that his proudest moment was when he 'buyed me the chocolate buttons'.

I Hate the Cinema

It was a chill late February, and the wind had culled a sea mist to a row of cafés struggling in their off-season to resist the onslaughts of the unfashionable cold and emptiness. Two women, one old and one young, were sitting in a glass corner of an otherwise deserted hotel café. A host of uniformed waiters, like matadors queueing for a turn at the bull, were hovering some twenty feet behind them. One or two desultory gulls took turns outside to swoop over the moored fishing boats, and the ranks of tethered pleasure craft. There was little coming and going on the narrow street. Some shops were open and selling bread or wine or cigarettes, but most of them seemed resigned to the fact that only a summer transfusion of tourists and sun could open their doors or unwind their shutters.

The wide flagstones outside the hotel were pale still with traces of the morning's frost. Beyond the street, a narrow esplanade and a rocky beach met the sea almost uneasily. Perhaps only the sea itself was unmoved by the plight of this small town on the Italian Riviera, incapable of surviving these dead months gracefully, but unable to conjure up any sun. The two women looked out from time to time from the porphyry mud of their congealed hot chocolates to the consistent blue of the sea.

They didn't know each other well. They had been drawn together by the emptiness of the place and by their own Englishness. They were like beached whales keeping each other company on a strange shore, lacking both the strength to leave and the will to stay. Every few minutes, sporadic attempts at conversation were made. Out on the beach, sheltered from the wind by the fortified base of a stuccoed church, two fishermen were mending their nets in defiance of the weather. There was an older and a younger man, each cobbling from one end of a wide net. Inside the hotel, the older woman stirred the dregs of her chocolate and then continued folding her napkin into what looked like a bird, while her companion tried to mend the holes of silence that hung stubbornly between them. Along the street, a faded poster beckoned to a long-forgotten film. Catching at the garbled colours, she spoke again, hopefully.

'How about the cinema?'

The older woman replied, suddenly vehement from inside her swathe of fur, 'I hate the cinema!'

Then she stopped folding the paper, and like a consummate actress she made the round rococo table her stage. With an almost imperceptible nod she brought two waiters to their corner and ordered Martinis. With a minimal shrug she slipped off her mink coat and seemed physically to ease her way into an unhealed memory. It was as though an undertow from her youth were dragging her away from her present idle opulence to a suppressed and impoverished past. Turning the large sapphire on her middle finger, she said, 'I was the youngest; with two sisters grown-up enough to love the cinema, but too young to do as they pleased. So they always had to ask my father if they could go, and he only had one answer – "If you take Mary along". That was me.'

She paused, narrowing her blue eyes a little, and realigned the mats and the ashtray.

'I was in the way. I was five and six and seven, and mother was ill. I think they hated me. I can still remember how they used to drag me down the street to those matinées, pulling my arms until they ached. If I cried, they pulled my hair.'

The younger woman wanted to say something, but she was stopped by a small gesture of the other's manicured hand.

'They weren't bad girls. But they had boyfriends, and their lives to live. I don't suppose it was easy for them either with mother in hospital, and father running the house like the barracks he had always lived in. I was just in the way.

'I didn't understand the films, or even put the names to faces. There was Douglas Fairbanks and Mary Pickford and Clark

Gable and a host of others that my sisters talked about, but I didn't know who they were.

'It was always dark in the cinema. I remember that was the worst. I was so scared of the dark. I used to cry, and then they'd pinch me till I stopped. Those films seemed to go on for hours and hours.

'I've never understood how anyone could go for pleasure and pay to sit in a dark hall and stare at those absurd transitory shadows.

'I used to pray all week not to have to go. But the girls were addicted. They always wanted to even though taking me was the price they had to pay for it. So they took me, settling all their scores on the way with pulls and pinches.'

Then she stopped talking as abruptly as she had started and turned now to her apéritif in its twisted-stem glass, and the small plate of olives and nuts that had been placed on their table. The younger woman looked up at her, wanting to hear more.

'How long was your mother ill?' she asked.

The older woman stopped poking the olives and paused with her cocktail fork in mid-air. She seemed both saddened and softened by the mention of the word. Then she stabbed a green olive on the plate and said, 'She was always ill. Always.'

They sat silently again, staring out to sea. There seemed to be no uneasiness between them now. The urge to talk had ebbed away and was gathering force again like the distant waves. Eventually the older woman pulled herself out of her reverie.

'She had TB, that was the cancer of those days. She was at home at first, but always lying down, resting. She never seemed to get better. It was as though she came home to get worse. Then she'd be back in the hospital, in the fever ward. I couldn't visit her there. It wasn't allowed. But they used to climb on to a wall, my father, I think, and an uncle, and they would hold me up against the bars of her window, and then I could see her in bed. Even as a tiny thing, I could hold on to those bars for hours.

'It didn't matter how ill she was, she never ran out of smiles for me. I was her favourite, her baby. I missed her every minute that she was away, but she always came back again. And then we had such wonderful times, it made up for all the other ones. She knew so many games and songs, you wouldn't believe how many; but I didn't need them. It was always enough just to sit in her lap – or to lie with my head on her pillow when she was too weak to sit up – and feel her near me.

'I can't remember when she wasn't ill. She used to spoil me. I think that made my sisters jealous. I was ten years younger than them, and they must have resented all the time I took away from mother. They knew she was dying, I didn't. I just knew that she had to keep going away but that she'd come back and cuddle me and keep me safe and they couldn't pinch me or drag me to the cinema when she was there. Even if they had done, nothing would have mattered if she had been there to go home to.

'She always wore white, white silk and white linen night-gowns, and her sheets were always clean and smelt of lavender from the bags she kept in the cupboards. I don't know how she ran the house from her sick-bed, but she did, even to the military standards that my father demanded. He wasn't always home. Sometimes he was away in the army. Once, I think he ran off with someone, but then he returned when I was about seven and stayed.

'I can remember the last time they put me on the ledge outside the fever ward. I was eight then, and nearly too big to cling to the sill. The other people in the beds around her always looked grey, but mother had a kind of radiance about her. They were mostly very thin, the women in that ward, and they seemed to glisten through the window. I remember that mother looked thinner than usual and, though she smiled when she saw me, I thought there was a heaviness in her look as though I had come at the wrong time. I had never felt that before. Even when she was coughing, at home, I was allowed to creep into the room and wait in a corner until she was well enough for me to hold her hand and stroke her hair. She had lovely hair.

'Father was in a hurry that day. He had been drinking and he wanted to get away. He told me to come down, but I wouldn't. We always did what father said. We had to. But just that once I wanted to stay, clinging to the bars of that first-floor ward looking in until mother's brow cleared at the sight of me. But it didn't that day.

'Everything seemed strange. Even father, instead of pulling me down and punishing me, let me stay, forcing my sisters to hold me up after he had gone.

'Mother and I could whisper things through the glass, lip-reading, and we talked in sign language. We used to say really silly things. That day, she seemed too sad to talk to me. It began to get dark and my arms were aching. The street lamps were already lit, and my sisters were frantic to be off by the time I finally climbed down. It was a long way back to the drab suburban terrace where we lived.

'That was the last time I saw my mother alive. She'd said that she would always come back. I believed her. She did come back one more time, still in white, but they put her in the parlour on the dining-room table extended with the middle piece. Some of her family came to pay their last respects, and they kept the coffin open all night. They used to do that, before the War.

'I sat with her, in the dark, all night. I had a chair with a high cushion so that I could reach over the edge of the box, and I held her hand. It was very hard, but still softer than not holding it. I can remember I felt happy with her, because she didn't look worried any more, and it was just the two of us like in our best times, and she had come back, like she said she would. I never could stand the dark, but that night it didn't bother me. I talked to her about all sorts of things, just chattering on. I don't know if anyone knew I was there. It never really mattered after mother died. I was just in the way and anyone was glad to see the back of me for five minutes.

'I was always fidgeting. I used to get into a lot of trouble for fidgeting. Mother used to call it "knitting magic" when I couldn't keep my fingers still.

'My sisters went as often as three times a week to the cinema.

'I hated it when they closed the coffin. I tried to stop them but I was dragged away and locked up in a room. I hated to think of her in the dark, with no air, and just those shadows with ghosts and cowboys and strange women and screaming men flitting over the lid.

'My sisters always sat in the middle row at the cinema. Whatever they did, they always did it in the middle row. There was something almost forbidden about the back seats, and the front ones were too visible. It used to terrify me when the lights went down.

'When the War came, I was fourteen. It felt like a release to me. The girls went off and did their bit, and father went back to his regiment, and I was alone. I'd been alone ever since mother died. I'd been alone for six years. But after the War came nobody ever dragged me to the cinema again, and the dark of the air-raid shelters was nothing compared to the dark of the Preston Astoria with its stale plush and its rows of giggling adolescents. I've never been back to see a film. Why would I? I hate the cinema.'

So saying, the older woman, who had, ironically, the decisive air of a retired film star, shouldered her coat. The younger woman said nothing. There seemed nothing to say as she stared out of the window on to the unchanging street bordering on the thin beach and the sea. A muffled tolling sounded from the church, and the two fishermen started, almost mechanically, to gather in their nets as a darkness began to creep over the small town.

The Shoes

The first pair was in Bologna, in a small boutique under the arcade that led from the station to the old square with the damaged statue shrouded for repair and the evening parade of young bloods in their finery. It was a tiny shop with only four shoes in the window, and the low black leather boot was one of them. The toe was slightly pointed and the sides rose in an Edwardian style.

Inside the narrow shop lettered boxes rose up to the intricately painted ceiling. It could have been an old chemist's by the look of it. But instead of apothecary labels gilded with Latin names there were just shoe styles and sizes.

The shoe was tried. There was only one pair left, and the hand-made size was right, fitting over the girl's leg to finish her arched black-stockinged foot in a demure flourish. Everyone admired her legs: they were unusually long, and so beautifully shaped that they raised spontaneous applause from old and young alike.

Until a week ago, she would not have dreamt of even trying on such a shoe. It was a luxury that could not even have been envisaged. Now, the price (two hundred and ninety weeks' pocket money) seemed irrelevant. The depth of her, or her mother's, purse had become unreal. So the cost of the tincture of arnica at the pharmacy for her bruises, and the many phials of essence of orange-flower for her nerves, and the cost of living away from home, in hotels, were no longer the budgeted holiday costs of other years but the necessary means of survival.

The shop assistant leant towards her, offering to help her on with the other shoe, but the girl shrank back and blushed, her wide dark eyes staring with a stunned wildness.

'They're not quite right,' she announced, 'not perfect.'

There was a pause, a waiting for a signal, and then the girl explained, 'They must be perfect.'

She was only fourteen, but nobody seeing her could have known that she was the daughter of the young woman beside her, or that the boyish man who escorted them both – though, somehow, most especially the girl – was in fact her mother's lover.

Once more, in the evening and under the burnished arcades, it was the girl who nestled under the young man's heavy opera cloak, and the mother who walked brooding but alert behind her. She walked two paces behind the long legs and the scant black mini-skirt and the chic tailored jacket of her frail child, staring at admiring passers by as though spoiling for a fight.

Every few steps the girl turned back to offer up her place of protection.

Later, in a café, they all talked about shoes. The girl knew just what she wanted. She would recognize them.

'I could identify them,' she said.

Until a week before, she could identify all that she wanted from life: the fame, the wealth, the flattery. She had culled them from her childhood and dreamed them into a fantasy so real that nothing else held much sway. The world would give her everything. She was young and beautiful. People admired her, painted her and photographed her. She wanted to be an actress, not to act, but to be a star. All the fourteen years of her life had moved towards it, gathering in the threads, like exquisite silk brocade, to this end. She had the confidence of a great lady and the flirtatiousness of a courtesan. When the fashion world 'featured' her, they were the lucky ones. The world was just a great machine working towards her dreams. It seemed that nothing could stop her, until a week ago, and the attack.

In seven minutes she had turned from victor to victim. Someone had raped her, leaving her battered and afraid of the very world she had thought she owned.

Nobody could see her cuts and bruises under her smart

unusual clothes. She herself no longer cared about the contusions themselves, it was the sheer violence of the act, the threats, the sick laughter of her attacker that filled her with despair. Every time the conversation stopped, her eyes sank back into a sadness that seemed to have no end.

All over Italy there were roadblocks out for the man who had attacked her. She had observed him well, the gold tooth, the mole, the concave forehead, the huge scar on his left hand. She could identify him. She knew just what he looked like, even though it had been dark.

Sometimes they talked of the ten years he would get when they caught him, if they caught him. Meanwhile he was at large, a maniac who had singled her out in a tiny village in Tuscany and broken into the house while she was there alone to rape and hurt her.

'He laughed. All the time he was doing it, he laughed.'

So the laughter of strangers became sinister. He was a man of about twenty-six, and all young men had become threatening. The firm land had gone from under her feet. She was afraid of the dark now, afraid of people, afraid to sleep, and dreaming had been all her life, before. The man had come to burgle her home, instead he had stolen her dreams. Only the shoes were left, and the shifting waters of Venice in her future. For months she had been told of the floating city where they would go to be together after Tuscany. They had all made plans with Venice at the pivot: an apartment for the lovers, and a tiny jewel for her: a studio with a balcony over a canal, a place of her own. A flat to herself in just one more year, somewhere to gather beautiful things around her. Venice had been such a new fantasy, it was, perhaps, the only one that couldn't drown under her new fears, but even it was tainted. The shoes alone existed as a pristine idea.

So the three of them paced through Bologna, the half-way mark between that village and Venice. They were within recalling distance of the Tuscan police. They could return if need be to rake over the grist, for an identification parade; or they could hide.

Their future depended on getting though the next few days, and the days were funnelled into the search for shoes. The city continued its life without even parting the traffic for their refugee clan. They moved through the shadows of old palaces as an incognito cortège.

It was two days to St Valentine's day and the streets were studded with flower stalls. Roses and violets and mimosas were carefully beribboned and on sale, but none of them bought any flowers. It was shoes or nothing for the grim triangle. The black that they all wore had slid from the fashionable to the funereal. The unspoken words in each of their heads were, 'Why me, why me, why me?'

The hours passed slowly, with each one paced out on paving-stones. At each café the girl would stroke the camouflaged discolourations on her neck.

'I was lucky, really,' she said, 'because he didn't tear my dress. You know how much I love it, and with the new shoes, I'll be like Lauren Bacall . . . No one will notice that I've been used. It'll be like before . . . And when I go to my premières and things, I'll stick my feet over the edge of the gondolas, and see my reflection in the sunlight on my shoes.'

Two days after St Valentine's day, footsore from hours of traipsing and searching, they were all in a restaurant in Venice. The identification parade had come and gone. The police had tracked down the wrong man, and the girl had released him. So all over Italy they continued to search for a dark man with a gold tooth and a mole and a scar and the other marks that made him the man.

Their own, private search had finished. The shoes had been found and bought and were now tapping sporadically under the damask table-cloth. The clockwork key that had threatened to wind them to breaking-point had been released.

Outside, it was night, and still, except for the occasional slapping of water against the canal wall. They all looked strangely dissipated as they clung with their eyes to each other and the pale raft of their table. Every few minutes they laughed, over-eagerly, as though tired of their grief.

Almost unconsciously, the girl bent down and removed a

shoe from her black-stockinged foot. A waiter came and cleared away the plates.

'I'm lucky, really,' she said, fondling the shiny leather, 'to have these beautiful shoes. I think we should go dancing.'

Miss Lizzie and the Musical Rats

Miss Lizzie is sitting on a train, leaning a little, on her blue upholstered seat, towards her small golden-haired daughter, who is asleep. East Anglia flits past her window, bearing its autumn colours as for some ancestral joust, and Miss Lizzie, feeling almost as resourceful as the Pilgrim Fathers, is on her way, not to America, but to the wilds of Norfolk. After months of wandering across Europe, spending a week in this hotel, and a week in that, she has finally found a place to escape to, a small haven for herself and her daughter. They always travel together, Miss Lizzie and her child. The mother, fleeing the phantom threats of custody orders, and the little girl, oblivious of being the cause of their patchwork life, setting up her small bag of toys and repacking them with the resignation of a born refugee.

Miss Lizzie, so named after a popular song, has been offered a safe place to stay in, a country cottage with an English country garden in a spot so isolated that no one in their right mind would go there. The train, halting now at Colchester, now at Manningtree and Woodbridge, cannot know that it is, today, not only a commuter service, but a vehicle of escape. It will take Miss Lizzie and her contended daughter to the end of its line, where a waiting taxi will drive them through the russet oaks of Hercules wood and on to the tiny huddle of cottages, two empty and one newly rented, for a year of rest and rural safety.

Everything goes according to plan, the taxi driver takes the two suitcases, everything that the young couple own now that their life has scattered what they once had like dandelion fluff from a used summer-clock, and drives them for an hour through the bright damp afternoon to the place where they are to live.

It has been raining in Norfolk. It usually rains in Norfolk, and
the rain has made the farm-track to her cottage impassable.
Miss Lizzie sees this only as an advantage, no one will find
them at the end of the half-mile of mud.

The cottage she is going to is like a stopping-place. Nobody
lives there for more than a year, it shelters one couple after
another as they pass on to other, more permanent abodes. On
either side of the slippery path there are fields of corn-stubble
spreading back in still tallow waves. The flat unbroken expanse
of stalks catches the last rays of the wintry sun, making the
land seem like an outsize scalp close-shorn with a blond crew
cut. There are no other houses or signs of life, nothing else to
see but the harvest's dregs, and a barbed wire fence, far away,
enclosing a coppice of trees. On the fence, hanging out to dry,
is the gamekeeper's laundry: a row of dead moles and mice and
weasels.

It is twilight when Miss Lizzie climbs the track. It is already
nearly dark ten minutes later when she reaches the rotten
wicket-gate of Dairy Cottages. Centuries before, they were the
making-place of butter and cheese; with rooms above for the
milkmaids to sleep in. Now, they are obsolete and neglected.
They have become quaint holiday cottages, locked up in the
winter and enjoyed in the summer by the extended network of
friends of the absentee owners. Sometimes a winter tenancy is
tried, but winters are bleak in Norfolk, and life itself is prey to
the winds. The wind drives any would-be dwellers away. It has
its own spectral way of entering the locked houses, it lives under
the timbers of the roof, and comes and goes as it pleases through
cracks in doors and the fissures around the small Georgian panes
of the windows. The wind holds forth in the wide chimney of
the ingle-nook, and it curls up and lodges in the narrow winding
chimney of the stove. In the garden it has bent the apple trees,
bowed down with mistletoe, and trampled the long, uncut
summer grass.

Miss Lizzie has been warned about the wind, she has ordered
firewood and coal to be delivered before her so that she can do
battle with the bane of Norfolk.

She leaves her heavy suitcases by the swinging gate, and
walks up the herring-boned brick path to the door. In one hand,

she holds the heavy iron key that will, very shortly, let her in to her home, in the other she holds her daughter's hand, squeezing the tiredness from it as she leads her over the bits of clinker trodden into the unweeded brick and the stunted windfall apples that crunch underfoot.

Miss Lizzie already knows what the inside of the cottage will look like, because she has seen it before, and remembers it from the time, years ago, when she visited a friend there. She could not have known then that she would one day need the temporary asylum of this stopping-place, so the details were not all there in her memory. But, the great ingle-nook fireplace with its carved mantel laden with plates, and the piano, and dresser, and chairs, the tables, the desk, the lay-out of the rooms, the feel of the antique furniture, the quaint clutter of auction-gathered miscellany was still clear. She knew that the place would have changed with the passing of time and tenants, just as she, too, had plans to change it; she would mend the broken window-pane, for a start.

What she could not have foreseen, as she turned the key in the big old-fashioned lock, was that the whole house had been vandalized. Every dish that could be broken was smashed on the floor, and every small piece of furniture overturned. Books and papers and sheets of music were torn and littered about, all the Victorian storage jars were destroyed, the cushions ripped, the upholstery torn, and under and over the strewn heaps of litter and dross, the blood and skins of dead animals were mangled and moulding. The smell was appalling; worse almost than the sight of the mess itself. The door was wedged half-shut and, as she forced it open, she heard again the shuffle that she had first heard on turning the lock.

Where Miss Lizzie might have felt fear, she felt only outrage, and she forced the door open, leaving her stunned and confused child outside. Whoever had dared to do this to her future home was not going to thwart her. She had travelled too long and too far. With the electric light on to guide her, and a heavy poker from the fire to protect her, she strode through the small cottage, kicking and slamming doors as she went. There were four rooms in all, four rooms and a pantry, and each of them had been the victim of the same petty destruction. To add to the chaos, there were rats in the house, she found their droppings everywhere, and had even seen several running over things. Much of the smell was their smell, the dank musty wretched odour of their filth.

In the wake of the chaos, only the rats were left. There was no other lurking intruder, no one to blame for having dared to wreck the four rooms of her dream. It was dark outside, and cold, almost as cold as the cottage itself with its accumulated damp and draughts. It was too late to go away, there was nowhere to go, at least that night. There was no telephone, no neighbour or village near, and no transport but her own tired feet. She had moved on too many times in the past year, stockpiling her imaginary fears while fleeing more real harassments . . . She had come to Norfolk to stay, and stay she would, whatever happened. She had nowhere else to go.

Her daughter's excited cries called her downstairs.

'Come and see, come and see, Miss Lizzie, look.'

Standing in the doorway, with half her slight body in the gaping windy night, and half her body illuminated by bright electric light, her child stood radiant with awe.

'Just look at them,' she whispered, and her mother looked at the half-circle of rats that had formed around her, staring, poised like a small army awaiting the signal to attack. The doormat seethed with the twitching grey fur. There might have been twenty or more, she couldn't tell, she had never seen so many together. For a moment, Miss Lizzie stayed paralysed with fear.

'Will they mind if I stroke them, will they like it?'

As the small hand reached out to touch, Miss Lizzie leapt from the stairs, shouting, as much to allay her own dread as to shoo the grouped rodents away. The grey band dispersed, the moment passed, and a slow return to order was achieved, at least in the country kitchen with its big fireplace, now lit, and its upturned stores.

After struggling with the fire, the first job had been to sweep everything to the floor and then sweep the floor itself. Miss Lizzie began the task willingly, rehearsing under her breath what she would say to the police on the following morning when she reported the break-in.

Every ten minutes or so the rats re-massed. She had grown so tired during the course of the day that her eyes were playing tricks with her. Once, when the rats gathered, it looked as though the entire staircase was filled with rodent reinforcements, undulating back into the two low bedrooms upstairs.

Each time they came, she shouted and hit out at them with her long broom, and they scattered, but kept returning. They seemed to have singled out her daughter, sniffing the young blood as they slunk across the brick floor to her, squeaking and scratching instructions to each other as to how best to surround her.

Long before she could bring herself to accept it, Miss Lizzie knew that it was the rats who had vandalized her home. It was they who had torn and chewed and overturned everything, it was they who had scattered the floor with mattress stuffing and dead creatures, these same rats who were hovering all around her, waiting to outwit her, to steal her daughter as soon as she fell asleep.

It was hard to think for the noise they were making, upstairs, crashing and thudding and squealing till Miss Lizzie's mind was blank with panic. She had heard how in the War, when the Germans bombed London, the main sewers had burst and the rats had escaped into the city, killing babies in their prams. And she had heard how they fought when they were cornered, to the death. But she was cornered, and she would fight, she would outwit them for this one night, and at daybreak she would seek help against the strange red-eyed invasion.

Miss Lizzie made a plan, and, keeping her child close by her at all times, she carried it out. Firstly, she built up the fire to a blaze and brought in piles of long wood from the outdoor shed. The rats were in the woodpile, they leapt out at her in the dark, they followed and darted, almost tripping her up. They were not afraid of her or the sticks she threw at them.

Back in the old kitchen, she stacked the fire with sticks, using them now to wave at the encroaching rodents. They were afraid of fire, she even hit some and burnt them and heard them shriek in pain, while the others rushed away.

The stairs were moving again, even through her tiredness she could see them clearly, heaving, not with dozens, but with hundreds of rats. To drown their noise, and to keep her courage up, she played music very loudly on the sixties record-player that she had moved near the sofa. All the furniture of the room she shifted, until only the sofa was left, like a small island by the fire with nothing close enough for a rat to jump from or climb up. Her child lay asleep on the sofa, covered with their clothes.

Outside the window, and round the chimney, and through the door, the wind sighed and wrestled in its dark night.

Miss Lizzie sat on the high sofa, with her feet doubled up under her, trying to draw comfort from the records she played between showering the waiting rats with sparks from her lit torch.

All through the evening she had been brave, with the bravery of young motherhood. Once her child was asleep, and no one could see, she wept on her besieged island. It was she who was afraid of rats. Her daughter had never before seen one and found them to have the natural attraction of all small furry animals, rating them somewhere between a hamster and a guinea-pig. It was the mother who feared the bare cord of their tails and the yellow stains of their teeth, it was Miss Lizzie who knew what the evil glint in their eyes meant as they crept towards her.

By midnight the rats had learnt that little ill came from Miss Lizzie's hot brands. They learnt to subdivide, leaving one column to bear the brunt of the fiery attack while another flank slipped round beside them to the sofa itself. Miss Lizzie learnt to throw hot ashes at them, and found a way of heaping red hot charcoal at the point furthest from her. Each time she put the needle back to the beginning of the record, she heard the wind wheeze in the garden. Each time the grey army of rats re-massed she found it harder and harder to keep them at bay. It was as though they bred upstairs in the intervals, coming down stronger and more numerous than before.

She found that, though they still shied clear of the fire, they liked the light. So she switched on the light at the back of the kitchen, by the wrecked pantry, and went back to her island in the dark, lit now only by the flickering flames and the red brigades of eyes. It occurred to her that they liked the music, too. Once, when she spilt some hot ash on to the record on the turntable, and had to change it for another, she thought the rats responded differently, holding back from the rock and roll as though that, too, could burn them. Experimenting gave her something to do. It kept her awake. More even than the rats themselves she feared her own falling asleep.

Whoever had last stayed at Dairy Cottages had been a fan of The Rolling Stones. She played one album after another, while the rats receded of their own accord during certain songs. All through the night, Miss Lizzie had prayed for help, and, though she had few beliefs, she begged for a miracle, for someone to come along the lonely muddy track and find her, for the rats to tire, for anything, if only she and her child could survive the night. All the things that she had been warned about, the wind and the rain, the cold and the isolation seemed as nothing now, if only the rats would leave them alone, if only the dawn would break so that they could go for help.

It was in the small hours of the morning when the incoming tide of rodents turned away, and Miss Lizzie knew that if she could only manage to stay awake, she could win. With the volume on full-blast, she had found a track that so disturbed the rats that they kept to the stairs. It was 'Ruby Tuesday'. It had an instant effect on them. They writhed and retreated. For hour after hour she played the doleful sad song and the vigilant vicious surge held back, in the macabre discotheque of her kitchen with their eyes catching the firelight and reflecting it in wild red and yellow lights, live strobes, twisting bulbs in the night.

Dawn broke slowly, a grey morning over the flat fields. At half past seven, two figures could be seen walking down the herring-bone of bricks, the one haggard and elated by the cold dull air, the other whimpering and out-of-sorts at having been pulled out of her sleep. Behind them, a small grey creature was climbing vertically up the outside wall, and disappeared through one of the many broken panes of an upstairs window. In front of them, an early frost was bracing each blade of grass that led down the uneven track to the road. It was two miles to the nearest telephone, three to the only shop.

It had been hard to keep the rats at bay that night. It was almost as hard to get anyone to believe in them at the Department of Health and Social Security. One phone call after another took place from the lonely freezing call-box, as Miss Lizzie tried to explain what was happening. Each time she spoke of a child in danger, she heard the phone being passed on with a whispered, 'You deal with her, she's mad.'

With threats and tears she finally got through to the rat-catcher himself, and he, at least, recognized some of the symptoms of her plague.

'Could be a stopping place,' he said, and arranged to meet her at the end of the track at one o'clock that day.

Miss Lizzie took her child into the village shop and bought food and ate it. Then she lingered there for a long time trying to find a way to verbalize her recent ordeal. Yet, even as she phrased the words in her own head they sounded so preposterous that she thought it better to keep what she knew of the rats to herself in the village, lest, in some way, she become tainted by association and ostracized later. The house and the five scattered cottages that made up the village seemed uninviting enough without her arriving unannounced and unintroduced with tales that seemed more fitting to a medieval chronicle than to a civilized home. The rat-catcher was coming, and he would deal with them, kill them, and they would never bother her again.

Already, with the chill mist of a morning between her and the nightmare of the night, the terror and the panic had receded.

All the way up the sodden track she told the rat-catcher what had happened. He was short and fat, and in his mid-fifties with balding hair and red, wind-lashed cheeks. His breathing came irregularly as he trudged up the path, and he kept staring into the stubbly field as though he had lost something there, long ago, but still hoped to find it. He spoke very little as he walked, nodding now and again indulgently, and merely adding to Miss Lizzie's narrative an occasional, 'People nowadays don't like rats,' as though, at some time in the past they had.

Outside the front door of Dairy Cottages there was the heap of cleared debris from the evening before. He stopped to examine this and then nodded again.

'Thought they might be mice,' he said, 'but them's rats.'

Inside, the fire had died to ashes, and the sofa looked bizarre on its own in the bared centre of the floor, with the gramophone squatting beside it, and the corpses of the night, fifteen in all, burnt and singed and stretched out at the foot of the stairs and against the pantry door. The rat-catcher looked at Miss Lizzie a little resentfully on seeing the first dead specimen, as though she had cheated him of what was rightfully his. On seeing all the others beyond it, he whistled under his breath and looked at her with new eyes full of approval, before setting out to reconnoitre the cottage and its sheds. Miss Lizzie followed him just far enough to keep him in her sight, feeling safer that way. Now that he had come, the living swarm seemed to have disappeared, and she felt obliged to tell him again that there were actually hundreds of them there.

'I see the signs,' he said, with satisfaction.

Miss Lizzie sat by her fire, stirring a pot of stew over it to the time of 'Ruby Tuesday'. The kitchen was scrubbed and clean, bleached in its every corner. All around her she could hear the excited chatter of grey furred creatures squabbling to feed at the trough. They need not have bickered, though, there was enough for all of them. The rat-catcher had laid enough poisoned bait to eliminate a thousand rats. Miss Lizzie had erected a makeshift chicken-wire fence around her sofa island, and her daughter was playing dominoes on a board on the floor inside it. The rat-catcher had warned Miss Lizzie 'You'd best stay away for a couple of days, stay with family or friends, till I get them all.'

Miss Lizzie had nodded, knowing that her friends were as scattered as the husks of the corn from the field outside. She could pack up her two suitcases and return to Europe, on the hotel circuit that she knew so well, or she could stay where she was, hidden from her pursuers at the mercy of the ravenous rats. Maybe she should have gone, she thought, but the worst was over and the house was full of traps and bait, she had passed the climax and now only had to weather the return to normal, like a patient recovering from brain fever, her crisis was over.

There were trinkets hanging from the wire fence like so many amulets: there was a set of tiny bells and bits of silver foil and saucepan lids and anything else that would jangle should the rats attempt to climb over it. The protective fence only rang twice in the night, and each time it was just a single inquisitive creature who had attempted to climb it. The others were busy with their grain. Miss Lizzie and her child slept fitfully, both disturbed by the storm outside. The wind was howling and sighing and wheezing in such a way that it seemed to surround them from inside the room.

Once again, Miss Lizzie was pleased when morning came. The rat-catcher would be back at eight o'clock to empty his traps and re-lay the bait. She knew that several of the traps had sprung, she had heard them in the night. She stayed huddled under the quilt of their clothes cradling her daughter's head until the rat-catcher arrived. She was squeamish, she didn't want to see the traps. The sight of the rats she'd burnt the night before had turned her stomach. She lay on the sofa looking out at the waving branches of the battered apple trees and thinking about her life and how it could have come to change so much that she should be where she was, alone but for the armful beside her. A plump, worm-eaten apple fell from the tree outside; she fell into a reverie about the inconstancy of things, and the wind wheezed its agreement.

Another day had passed, the rat-catcher had come and filled his rat bag with twenty stiff grey corpses, some with their backs broken in the traps, but most of them glutted on the poison grain. In the afternoon, he had returned, and cleared away another dozen victims of his zeal. Miss Lizzie had made a bonfire on the grass and burnt the mattresses that the rats had been in, and the cushions and all other spongy things. Some of them were already heavy with dead rats, the greedy ones, who had eaten most grain. After the bonfire came a mammoth wash, with sheets and blankets bleached in the bath tub and then hung out to dry. The rain had stopped, and the wind had dropped, leaving only a strange residual sighing in the house, like a whispered appeal from within the cavity walls.

That night, the cottage seemed almost habitable, despite the fence and the sofa which still served as a bed for both of them. And yet Miss Lizzie could not sleep. She had worked until late clearing and cleaning, bracing herself to remove the stiff bodies of the dead rats that she now found everywhere. There wasn't a drawer or box or cupboard that they had not crawled into to die. She had a long shovel and a pair of gloves, and with these she filled the rat-bag on the roof of the low lean-to shed.

It was as though she had had the gentleness torn out of her. She felt no pity for the curled hand-like claws, or the long repulsive tails. She looked calmly at the dozens of glazed eyes as she scooped the bodies out of their hiding-places, wondering by what process pity dies. She had never seen herself before in the role of an exterminator, but such she had become, gloating over her tally, glad at their deaths. The rat-catcher would be back in the morning, marvelling at the quantity of corpses like a connoisseur, probing their pale yellowy bellies with his stick. He had told her a great deal about them. Some of it Miss Lizzie had found reassuring, some of it she had wished he had kept to himself.

For instance, it was better to know that there was nothing personal in this particular rodent attack. It was 'a phenomenum', the rat catcher had said. He said it as though 'a phenomenum' was all right.

'It's just the second time I've seen it in my lifetime,' he said, 'this sort of thing. I've heard about it though, they just get up and go sometimes, gathering from all over the county, and they come together at a stopping-place, like holding a meeting, and they all know where to go, and they march by the hundred to it, and they stay a while, and then they go, scattered, nobody knows where. It's a phenomenum, and this . . . is a stopping-place all right, no doubt about it.'

What she hadn't liked was the description of the poison, specially designed to avoid the dreadful smell of a dead rat.

'It dehydrates them, so it does, from the lungs out. It's a bit slow at times, and it makes them gasp, but if you miss one, even in a mattress, you won't ever smell a thing: dry as a bit of old leather they are.'

That was when she had burnt the mattresses.

It was getting late, very late, and Miss Lizzie was tired, but she couldn't sleep. The walls disturbed her, the house was sighing so much it was keeping her awake. She clambered over her fence and went and stood in the garden for a minute. It was quiet out there except for the distant calling of an owl. The wind had gone from outside, it was only in the cottage now. She went back in, listening, straining every nerve to discover what exactly was distressing her so. The whole cottage was haunted by the sound. It almost seemed to whisper her name, over and over, with a slurred, gasping, rasping appeal of pain and desperation. It was like the wheezing of her own asthma transferred to the fabric of the house. At least when the rats had tried to attack her she had been able to fight them back. To think that she had imagined that night as the worst. Now her brain began to hurt with the dull ache of the interminable sighing, wheezing, sighing. The rats were dying inside the cavity wall and between the floorboards and the ceiling. Dozens and dozens of them had crawled in there to die, and now they were, slowly, in an agony of dehydration, gasping through their damaged lungs for breath.

For three nights more the wheezing continued, and for three days, and then all was still. The rats had lost their hold on their chosen stopping-place, and with their passing, Miss Lizzie had lost the hold on her head. The wind that had sighed and wheezed and turned to drying flesh between her walls had returned and carried the sound away again. So, the rats were gone, but the wind kept coming back, was almost always there, and Miss Lizzie was afraid of its whispering. The sound of it in the night woke her up in alarm, seeing red-eyed vermin crawling on her bed while hearing the slow chorus of their accusations. The rats' pathetic crying had crept into her head and lodged there, somewhere at the back, in a spot that seemed bare and unprotected. Each time the wind drove round her apple trees she felt as though trepanned by fear and guilt. She understood the fear, it was only natural, but why the guilt? The voices had called her name, 'Missss Lisssie', they had singled her out, they had cried for days and days, begging her to ease the pain, walled in, unable to live or die. All this and more was walled inside Miss Lizzie's head.

She stayed in Norfolk with her child, and the child grew and seemed to forget everything about the rats except for the one song, 'Ruby Tuesday'. Poor Miss Lizzie can't forget. The wind won't let her. She wonders, sometimes, 'How long will the wind blow?' The wind always blows in Norfolk. Yes, but how long will it sigh and wheeze? It has no other way, it always sighs, passing on the sighs it gathers as it goes by. By the fireside, and by the apple trees and by the gate, it is the same, always whispering her name. 'Why does it keep saying my name?' Miss Lizzie cries into the night. It's just sighing, Misss Lizzie, just sighing.

Hail Mary full of Grace

Even your friends were afraid of your eyes; your green Antarctic eyes. You could strip me of my flesh; my hair; my will; but the bones that were left were always big bones, too big. I used to think you were a witch, mother, and you used to say I was in the way: an unwanted alien who shamed you with her presence and the vulgarity of her hair. I had red hair: tainted hair.

You were frail and five foot tall and clairvoyant. From within my growing loneliness I saw that there were so many people who loved you, and you never even tried to reel them in or keep them close. You ruled by your indifference and the flashes of manic passion under your cold exterior. Granny loved you despite your rages. She seemed to know of secret ways to reach behind your bitterness. You accepted her. I don't know who you loved, though, it was too hard to tell. Only your disfavour was clear, and I stood out in it; like an abandoned spire.

You married my father in 1919. He was a soldier hell-bent on forgetting the War and you were a pampered young beauty. If you hated anyone more than me, it was him. You never forgave him for the greatest crime of all (in your eyes): he took you to a place that bored you. You were almost as afraid of boredom as I was of you. So you ran away from my father, and Canada, and returned to Jersey as a refugee with only your inquisitorial powers and an unwanted pregnancy for luggage. Granny never quite forgave you for having planned to abort me. She called it divine intervention when your ship was delayed and rerouted through winter storms. You arrived too late for an abortion. So I was born on the wrong side of your favour into our Catholic family.

Your own father, who had spoilt you, was newly dead and the family ruined by his gambling debts, but you blamed me for all your misfortunes. You were so incensed by my birth that you refused to name me. It was Granny who called me Joan, for St Joan canonized that year, and Mary, for Our Lady, and for you, mother. I don't think you ever touched me save in anger. I know that I never saw beyond my own anger to your despair.

If I keep scratching at my bitterness, it all comes down to that failed abortion, and the hint of death in your eyes. There was never any hint of travelling to foreign lands or hopes of handsome strangers in your premonitions, mother; just death, and the time and place of its arrival. Instead of a shell, I had the grudging tarpaulin of our home; and you seemed to need to keep taking that away from me. It wasn't enough that I should be exiled from your emotions: there had to be punishment as well.

If I close my own eyes hard enough, I can understand some of your rage. You must have felt frustration at the inevitability of the deaths you could foretell: your courtiers were dying while my own life stretched interminably ahead. Perhaps it was seeing my sixty years staked out in front of me, and yourself, shackled by association to those six decades that angered you. If I had been small and graceful, with emerald eyes like your own, I wonder if you'd have forgiven me. But then no one could have eyes like yours, and I was born huge and doomed to grow and grow.

When I was five, you remarried. He was a Yorkshireman, a country gentleman who used to come for me sometimes in his latest Rolls-Royce, to the door of Mrs Sidebottom's dancing class. I remember that she insisted on being called 'Seedybottome' with the accent on the last syllable. And I remember you, mother, sitting reluctantly by his side, with your only greeting of 'you are staring, child', and the petulant stamp of your tiny foot on the carpeted floor of the car. I used to stare out of fear and hope. You just stared.

Granny managed to save some money from the family crash.

She had a small income of her own which was what we lived on; first, in the house of one of her old Irish maids, then, later, in London. I think your natural spitefulness was warped by our poverty. Everything was sold, and the servants dismissed. Only a few mementoes of the failure were packed into trunks and cooped up in the attic with you and your growing bitterness. I was too young to remember those years before your remarriage, but I do remember that I was never allowed to be in the same room as you. I remember your voice, 'Keep her away from me!' and your glacial eyes.

I was your only child, the inevitable scapegoat of your disappointment and clumsy recipient of your dislike. I used to beat my fists against my bedroom wall so that God would make you love me. I said so many Hail Marys that they stuck in my head, and Granny said I said them in my sleep. It didn't make any difference, I was always 'keep her away from me' to my own mother, Mary. By the time I could say my Creed, and even before, when I mouthed in the middle range of 'I believes', I knew that red hair was a sin, and if you didn't love me, it was my own fault. I believed in the Holy Catholic Church, and our Father O'Hare, and in my blame. Later, much later, long after I had ceased to believe in God, I still believed in you.

When we moved to London, you to your soirées and your admirers, and I to the black gym slips of the German nuns, Granny told me that the convent would be for the best. Your anger seemed to increase in proportion to my height. The other girls railed against the Prussian discipline of our school, but I was immune to their torment. They never seemed half as cruel or capricious as you. For ten years I stayed in the convent, spending most of my holidays there too, at your own special request, while you gathered together the threads of your social life after what you always referred to as 'the disaster' of my birth. I learnt the harsh clumsy tongue of the nuns. And I learnt to accept their brass rulers on my knuckles at each wrong answer to their trick questions that came down like horseflies all through the summer. I thought of you a lot, mother, and I missed you all the time that I learnt to make the Nazi salute with my hockey stick there, and to compound my words.

Even going over these things leaves a stale taste like stewed turnips in my mouth. It is twelve o'clock now, and the lunch-trollies are coming round the ward. It is creamed chicken and tapioca: a soft diet for the softness on my spine. Most days I feel sick of this invalid's food. But now that I have you stuck like a lump in my throat, mother, I feel as though I couldn't swallow any real food again. In the past, you were so often there, like the blue paper of salt in my crisps, a twist of bitterness at the bottom of every packet. Long after your death, the thought of you could still damp all my pleasures; and the memory of your eyes could paralyse.

My back hurts; I think it hurts as yours must have done on the night of my birth. The doctor arrived late and drunk and forced your tiny frame to let me through. He crushed my skull with his forceps: the dents are still there. I knew that it was all my own fault: you told me so. In self-defence, I used to pretend to hate you too, but I still said my Hail Marys for it after confession until I was eighteen years old. I missed what I had never known. Even though you could not love me; I wanted you to forgive. It was not your way, to relent; instead, your antipathy grew as surely as this cancer on my spine.

I left home the moment I felt able to defy you. It was on my eighteenth birthday, and you hit me for the last time, reaching up as you had had to do for years. The War was coming, and I became a nurse, and neither liked the work nor found much freedom in it. I only had Sundays off from the teaching hospital, and every Sunday I went to visit Granny in her nursing home in Chislehurst. She was crippled by cancer in her hip. I saw her every week until she died, but I never saw you again.

You could summon the living and the dead to you. Most of all, though, you could make people do what you wanted. I want you to come back to me now, mother. I'm willing you back to me, but I don't have your powers. You used to say to Granny,

'Do you know, I can't get so and so off my mind,' and within the week, so and so would die. Friends and family and strangers all fell into your web. You never seemed to care. You were a witch, a beautiful cruel witch, and we were so bad for each other. I can see you now, with your lace and your terrifying eyes, and your rose-water, getting ready for a house-party at the de Gruchys' or a dance at the Mosleys'. I remember you sipping orange-flower water for your nerves and tapping your fan with rage on the veneer of your dressing-table while our one skivvy did your hair. You must have known how you frightened her. Did it amuse you or didn't you care?

If the tumour on my back had been a fraction to the right it could have all been cut away; and then my legs would move again, and the cold spot on my spine could thaw. And if only you had smiled at me once, mother, things might have been different. But you didn't, and they aren't. Is it your stare, like a laser beam, that's pinning me down to this bed? Are you here somewhere in the ward with me?

I often think of you, mother: if I close my eyes, when I'm tired, I can still see yours. I had four marriages, you know, and they all ended the same, with or without the War, impaled on my own fear of rejection. There were four husbands, and four children, and nothing to protect me from the malign force of your thoughts but the thin veil of my tears. I cried a lot to protect myself from your absent stare.

One night, in 1953, I lay awake in bed, and I think I heard you die. It was as though I heard you call to me, digging into my brain as only you could. I buried my good ear in my pillow and blocked you out. I refused to hear you then. I thought I hated you, so I refused to hear, and now, all these years later, I'm calling you. I want to see you again before I die, I want to see whatever Granny saw hiding under your bitterness.

It wasn't until long after the War that I learnt to calm down and control myself. I had stopped banging my fists against the wall before I found out that you'd died, but not even your death could ease my anxiety. It always hurt me that I wasn't like you. You might have loved me if I'd been smaller and less doggedly sad. Gradually, I grew from being 'poor plain Joan' into something much admired. People called me beautiful, but for me, I was still too tall and clumsy, and not at all like you. I tried, but I knew, even as a child, that trying wasn't enough. I'm making amends, though, mother, more even than by Hail Marys. I've willed myself to die, just like you could.

Sometimes I think the whispering in the ward at night sounds very Catholic. Perhaps that's why I think so much about you. You were my religion for so many years. I asked Father O'Hare once how I could find favour in the eyes of God, and he told me, 'First you must find favour in your mother's eyes.' It would have pleased you, mother, Mary, to know how much you denied me. Not many women can take away a Church.

I don't want to die hating you. I don't want to die in sin. After sixty years of bitterness, it's here, in this last month of lying down, that I've thought of you for the first time almost with affection. I could only ever see my own side of our feud before. Now I wake up in the night and I can't get you off my mind. Here, in this thin bed, wheeled from the window to the nurses' desk, squeezed in between the old women dying, I've found a kind of creed again, after forty years of faithlessness. I believe in *you*, the mother I hated, maker of beauty and despair. And I believe in the forgiveness of sins.

Can you forgive me, mother, you who were blessed among women? O, and let me not be ashamed. Even on holiday, at Selsey, when you were asleep on the beach, I felt you criticize me for being alive. It was always me to blame, always mea culpa, mother. I've never known till now how to earn your forgiveness. But I've been practising your powers, and I think I can see my own death; and I feel drawn towards you.

Granny died of the cancer in her hip. You died in an asylum, more alone even than I with my tumour. I think I would have helped to burn you, years ago, and gladly lit the fire around your stake with my own flaming hair. But no more. I've changed. I want to know you now. I've never known you. Why were you certified? Was it because of your green eyes, so green they paralysed? Tell me, mother. I hear whispering all over the ward, but I can't pick out your voice. Would you forgive me if I died?

Anne of the Ragged Lace

Anne

Summer always came late to the fens, it was mostly water there, and mist and mud. The sun can rise and set over the fields and flood-drains in The Saints, and people hardly notice it. It would have taken more than that pale sun to stir the solid surface of our village. I used to like to look up at that frail disc in the sky. Grandad said it was dangerous to stare at the sun. He said you could go blind. But he'd been out in India, and it must have been different there. The only fire in our sky was diluted and as colourless as I, with my too blonde hair and my too pale skin. I'm quite strong, though; I just look weak.

I loved the way the sunlight was sifted through the clouds into pale streaks. I liked them best filtered through the ragged patterns of the cow-parsley, the Queen Anne's lace that grew as thick as planted barley. Whenever I lay down under the canopy of flowers, I felt I was in my world, a queen, at last, in all her finery. 'Anne of the ragged lace' was what my grandad called me.

I'd go missing from the village, and I'd always be there, on the bank of the thin brown river, lying under the white parasols of flowers. It bound me to the village: my title, and the magic growth of stalks and leaves and the white haze. Whatever lacked in me, I found in them. I didn't talk much about my discovery. I told my grandad, and Tommy, and that was all.

Most of the village talk was about stoves and beet and

barley, and water levels and the bus times to Lynn. Or it was about boys and clothes and Saturday outings. Sometimes we talked about swish jobs over the horizon, knowing that there could be nothing there because The Saints were so flat and no one had gone beyond them, except old soldiers. Yet the talk continued, and every boy in The Saints cut a vicarious dash describing this or that detail of his luxury flat-to-be in the city. The fantasy was part of our chemistry, as important to the village as the Spar supermarket or running water or soap operas.

The only things that actually happened in the village took place on television or in the back of a car, or, much more usually, behind the bus stop. The seasons came and went so slowly that few of us noticed the change. There'd be a new baby at Hangar Lane, or a funeral from Number Five. They were just the natural things of a place given over to reaping and sowing.

In every front room or kitchen, the television spoke as from another planet. Our world was guided by 'the box'. When we weren't watching it, we discussed its goings on at the bus shelter, 'the stop'. It stood out on the windiest part at the edge of the housing estate. It was like a boat in a sea of mud. It was our life-support. The two lurching double deckers that passed there twice a day were almost irrelevant to its importance. Life was not what lay beyond our windswept huddle of houses, it was life as discussed, observed or brooded on from the stop. Nothing ever changed, it just slowly mutated towards its inevitable return to the dark clay around us.

I was born there, on Hangar Lane, and I grew up there, like we all did, sorting out and discarding the twentieth century from the grim safety of the bus stop. No one ever questioned the way we lived, or tried to break away or even disrupt it, no one, that is, until Tommy. I used to think that as long as the ragged lace continued to flower, year after year, I would be happy staying there, having a cottage of my own, or one of the new bungalows, and a family, competing a little with my friends, and doing things well. I belonged there, in The Saints' country, between the five churches that we rarely used: St Peter's, St German's, St Mary the Virgin, St Mary Magdalen and St Clement's. I loved it more than anything except Tommy Watkins.

I'd known Tommy all my life, and I'd watched him growing away from us all like a giant hogweed in a patch of beet. We went to school together, and read the same books and poems and failed the same geography exams, but the words were different inside my head. They were always different, and so was Tommy, but no one minded because everyone had their ways. Mine were with the flowers. Johnny Gotobed had a kitchen garden full of fridges; dozens of them rusting into heaps like sculptured shrubs, and none of them working or ever would. Harry kept ferrets, and slept with them in his bed; and even Mum had a thing about folding. So, when Tommy took to his drums, nobody cared. He still met his mates at the stop.

His drumming always reached its peak in the summer, and gradually it began to compete with my collaged skies. At other times the north-easterly winds drowned out his restless pounding. All The Saints' country lived a prey to the wind, so no wonder Tommy couldn't compete with it. Not that he didn't think he could. Tommy thought that everything had been created expressly to set him off, even the wind and the rain. I can't remember when I started to believe it too, but I did.

Tommy was always popular, especially with the girls. Not even my own folk could understand why he had his eye on me. They used to joke that I was only half-made. Me being the eldest, they said they hadn't got the hang of how to make babies when it came to me, and that was why I'd turned out so insipid. The only thing I ever had to boast of was my closeness to the Queen Anne's lace and Tommy. It made me special, special enough to have been happy there in The Saints for always.

Every day Tommy grew more restless to get away. He hated Hangar Lane, hated The Saints, even the fens themselves. I never understood that, because I loved them. But then I never understood him, and I loved him too. He was obsessed by the city. It wasn't even Lynn he wanted, it was London. He said that he despised Lynn. He actually wanted to go to London.

He wanted to be a star. When he talked of it, his eyes changed colour, from dull brown to clear.

'Can't you see it?' he'd say.

I couldn't, I had my world, my place, my ragged lace. To go to the city seemed as likely a thing to do as to climb inside a television set and block out the characters with my bulk. But he talked sweet words to me, and he stroked my hair. My mum used to stroke my hair as well, but she used to touch it with a kind of wonder, that she, who was so complete, could have produced me, who wasn't. Sometimes, when she started folding, I used to think that her lips weren't pursed against dad's old jokes any more, but brooding on the transparency of my hair and the paleness of my eyes. My brothers used to call me red eyes, because I cried a lot and it made me look like an albino. Tommy never called me that, he didn't even see it. I was his princess, heiress to the kingdom of Queen Anne's lace.

I had my long plantations of feathery leaves, and my ivory brocade of petal stars so I didn't need the rhythm of other people's drums. Tommy used to say that what I had was too ephemeral to be real. I didn't know what I had, except that it was what I wanted. And then, suddenly, it wasn't enough, although nothing much had changed. I suppose nothing ever changed in The Saints, or could, or would. It was just a landscape of mildew and mud into which the pale sun dripped its filtered sweetness intravenously, and I carried some of its sweetness in my blood.

The last summer before I left The Saints, I lay under the highest Queen Anne's lace by the river, and all I could think of was Tommy, Tommy, Tommy and pray to the tall stalks that he wouldn't go away.

Tommy

I was born here, but I hate it. I started drumming to annoy my dad. That's how I found out I was a drummer. I'd always been a dreamer. For years it was the drums that kept me going, that and hearing the daily calls for Anne of the ragged lace. She used to lose herself in the fields, and I loved hearing them all hunting for her, calling her name, like a character from a play. I used to dream about her. She'd be my queen, and I'd be the greatest rock star in the world with all of London at my feet and my pale lover in tow, paler than anyone, and smiling with whatever secret it was that she culled from the fields.

She never really understood what glitter was about. It was all pale sun with her, and that killed me. If she'd stayed in The Saints, they would have swallowed her up, put her to sleep, planted and gathered her until there was nothing left but husk. Every autumn, when my dad dug the garden, I felt he was burying me bit by bit in his clay. And what I hated him for most was he couldn't even see he was doing it. He was always so bloody ready to talk and change, so understanding, but he didn't understand the first thing. When they heard from somewhere that I wanted to go to the city, they started bunging me full of some government training scheme.

If I hadn't been born in the fens, things would have been different. Its mud sticks. I knew that if I played hard enough, loud enough, someone would hear me and give me a break. That was all I needed, just one break and everything would have been different, one break from the city. The trouble was, people could see that I came from the fens. I didn't belong there, ever, but it must be like having webbed feet or something, real city people can just look at you and tell.

I mean, we're almost into the twenty-first century. People have space ships and Porsches. The days of the hoe are over. Stuff the sugar beets. I hate them. I never eat sugar. I gave it up when I was eight – I didn't want any part of it. Oh, and then the highlight of the week, the one that we were supposed to look forward to, a trip to the dole office on the bus, a beer, a game of darts and six more evenings hanging round the shelter. Even during the War people used to crawl under their shelters and something would happen on top. Dad used to say, 'It's not like that, son, you've got lots of alternatives.' And of course, I had. I could have worked in the sugar beet factory, been a success, and dug my garden, like my dad.

*   *   *

Tom tom tom tom. I tried to raze The Saints, I hated them. I was in love with Anne of the ragged lace. I tried to explain how things were, but she just didn't understand. She'd got this thing about belonging on the land and nothing changing. She wasn't thick, just brainwashed. There was no way I was going to vegetate. I'd have gone anyway, even if I hadn't got my talent.

Anne

I had to go, Tommy would have gone without me. I tried to tell my mum, but I couldn't turn it into the kind of words she'd understand. I wanted to tell my dad as well, but I knew he'd say, 'Sixteen and no job is no good in London.' He'd have tried to stop me, and I didn't want to hurt him, because I had to go. Tommy said in six months we'd have a big apartment and he'd be signed up with a record company, and I'd have a wardrobe like Krystle in 'Dynasty'. I didn't want that, though, not any of it, just Tommy. He had a mate in London, someone who'd come to The Saints for holidays, and we went to stay with him in Notting Hill Gate.

I'd never seen so many faces or so many motors. Tommy said the fens were grey, and yet the day we got to London, I felt a greyness crawl all over me, and it has never gone away. Even my hair picked up the grime. It was like another country. I didn't have the heart to say much, and I didn't need to, because Tommy talked enough for everyone, describing the band he was going to form, and the gear they were going to wear, how often they'd go on tour, and that sort of thing.

His friend didn't like me, he said I gave him the willies, being so pale and quiet. Tommy used to call him Boxer. I don't know if that was his name, he didn't look strong enough to be a boxer. He was more of a traveller, really. He told Tommy he was going to the Philippines soon, he talked about it a lot. He had a poster over his bed of a place called Jakarta. I tried to like Boxer because he looked after Tommy. He knew that the one thing that made Tommy nervous was sticking out in the city, so he helped him to merge in. He even gave him some of his H for free and he never charged us rent. I tried to imagine what mum would do if two people turned up on her doorstep. She would probably have done the airing cupboard a couple of times and then folded herself in despair.

Tommy kept telling me that I wasn't trying to be nice to Boxer. I suppose he complained about it. He just made me feel uneasy, and although he was helping Tommy, it seemed that he was just changing him into someone I understood even less than I had before. Tommy said that was what happened in the city; people changed and things started to happen and that was right. That was what we had come for. Boxer even changed my name. He said that Queen Anne of the ragged lace was hick, and he changed it to Queer Gladys. Somehow, that was the one that stuck: it became my city name.

That was the first summer that Tommy couldn't play. Boxer was worse than his father. He hated drumming and noise in general, and Tommy's in particular. I thought that Tommy would be lost without his drums, I hoped it would make him feel as lost as me, so that we could go home. But he said it didn't matter. It was better to absorb our surroundings, change our style, drop the hick. For music, we used to go to Waterloo to hear the buskers, and I would watch the dirty water swirling under the bridge.

Tommy

There are ways into a city, it's like crawling into a wasp's nest really. You have to know how to do it. How not to stand out for the wrong reasons. I should have gone to the city on my own. It was a responsibility being in love, a liability. Anne kept saying that we should go back to The Saints, and she shouldn't have said that. Saying things can make them happen. It alters the pattern, changes the rhythm. It's a jinx. Even thinking things is like that. It's like with murder: there is malice aforethought.

We had to grow a new skin. Boxer didn't really understand me either, which was strange, considering he understood such a lot. Boxer was a travelling man. He said travel stretches your awareness. Well, I know it does. I mean, we got out of the fens and it changed our whole perception. But we weren't hicks, not inside. And I'm not just saying this, but I'm good on the drums. Better than good, I'd say, bloody brilliant. We had to pawn the set, and I miss them. I just rattle out my ideas now on Coca-Cola cans.

If Boxer had really listened to my music, I just know he would have felt differently about us. I mean, nobody tells Mick Jagger who to screw. Boxer kept telling me to ditch Anne/Gladys. He said I was a loner. He was wrong though, I needed Anne, and I've never liked being on my own. I get bad dreams. I used to get them at home. An artist needs his public. Anne of the ragged lace used to be my best fan. What kind of a name is Gladys? It sounds more like my gran.

She and her cronies have to be the most boring morons ever born, but they did have something with all their yakking about the War, and waiting for years for their soldiers to return. You'd think Anne could have had a bit more loyalty; stood by me; tried. But no, she just turned out as bad as all the rest, spoonfed on telly. She expected everything to happen in one go. You have to sink to its depths to know what life's about. You go down, and then you go up. I could have made it if she'd had more guts. It was my day. I could feel it coming, a big break was on the way.

Boxer was right, though. She was a watery person. She had the little thin mind of an eel. She started saying she didn't know me any more. She always nagged me about the H, she hated it. If she'd had an ounce of intelligence, she would have seen that H was just camouflage. It brought me friends. They didn't call me hick in the Underground. I could score and a whole load of people would say, 'Hey man, Tommy.'

They knew my name in the city! My own name. Strangers would talk to me like friends. Only Gladys, who was meant to be my best friend, went off me.

Nag nag nag. Nag nag nag. What did she expect? Of course it cost a lot to stay on H. No one was going to give me money if I asked them, it takes a girl to do that. I pawned my drums, for Christ's sake, what more did she want! The other girls did it at Waterloo, dozens of them. And Gladys got a lot of money when she set her mind to it, fifties, pounds, even fivers. But she didn't care if I was in pain. She'd turned against me by then. I could tell. I never thought she'd be like that. She used to be sort of different, nicer. Boxer tipped me off, right from the start, he said that queer Gladys was mean.

Anne

We started to make friends after Boxer chucked us out. We slept under the arches at the station. It was quite nice because it was warm and I'd always liked Waterloo. I liked the river, it reminded me of the fens. There were a lot of us there, and no one called me a kid or said I was too pale to stay with them. We were all pale there, I don't know if it was the hamburgers or the H, but everyone had an ashen look, even the dark ones. The city made everyone grey.

When it started to get cold, we used newspapers for blankets, and the print came off them and stained our skin. It made me feel really old being covered like that with yesterday's news.

Tommy said I didn't love him any more, but I did. He'd get really vicious when I didn't help him. He said that I'd lost faith in him just because we didn't have the apartment and he hadn't bought me any diamonds. He didn't seem to understand that I'd only ever wanted *him*. I just wanted to unpawn his drums. I told him he couldn't get a break without his drums, but he called me a hick and a moron.

We were the cream of the station. It was ours. Outside, under the bridge, all the old tramps and winos lived in cardboard boxes. We didn't mix with them, though. They used to stink.

There was a girl called Gail who did the ticket queues with me. She was my friend, she came from Dumfries. Gail said the station was like a hotel compared to where she came from, and she was going to stay there forever. The gangs came sometimes and stole all our things, but Gail said it didn't matter. Sometimes she'd even come to the Embankment Gardens with me, where there were flowers, but they didn't have any Queen Anne's lace. I asked about it, once, but a man told me it was only a weed, and they pull weeds out in the city. Gail was so nice to me that I told her my real name, and she said she thought it

was really pretty. Tommy never used it any more, he didn't
want his mates to think we were hicks.

I went down to the river every day. Tommy said it was
pathetic, at first, and then he changed his mind. He actually
made me go and get money from the bridge. Later, it was Gail
who told me that Tommy was carrying on with another girl.
Of course, I didn't believe her. All we had was each other,
Tommy and me, and Tommy's future.

When I first saw them together, I went to the Ladies' and
cried. Then I waited until he was on his own, and I asked him
why. He wouldn't talk to me. He said, 'Shut up, red eyes,' and
after that he just ignored me. I waited for a few days, sort of
hanging around and it was really embarrassing. We were living
in the same 'hotel', and we still had the same patch. I couldn't
move away, you had to fight to get your space. So I had to
watch them and hear them and it made me sick. The boy from
the heel-bar had a crush on me. He offered to look after me,
but I was in love with Tommy. I did take a fiver from him for
my bus-fare home. I didn't have the heart to beg, you see, not
for myself. I'd only ever done it for Tommy.

All the way back I kept my forehead pressed against the glass,
looking at the grey houses and then the rain and the mud and
the trees. It was December and I didn't know if my mum and
dad would want to see me. They liked Christmas. I didn't know
if I would spoil it for them, going home. But I thought that if
I had to freeze by a river I'd rather do it in The Saints, beside
the Ouse, with my own name.

I took the bus from Lynn, and they were glad when I came
home. Dad told me that I belonged there. I didn't tell the
Watkins about Tommy. I said I didn't know where he'd gone.
Then I waited, all winter, for my flowers. No winter has ever
felt so long. I didn't go to the stop any more, even though my
old mates all invited me. They treated me like someone famous,
and they didn't call me red eyes again, but nothing else seemed
to have changed. The fens still stretched out into the clouds,
and I could see for miles. I could count the square towers of
three of the five churches.

I'm sure mum thought I was pregnant because she perked up

when the months passed and she could see that I wasn't. And she didn't sigh too much, or push me to get work at the beet factory, and Dad was very sweet to me. He kept telling me that the cow-parsley would be up soon. He knew that I was waiting, just waiting for my life to come back to me. Marking time. When the first leaves came through in April, and then the first flowers, in May, I knew I would survive. But, when summer came, and the lace made a high haze along the river-bank, I realized that my old pleasure was gone. I was no longer queen of the fields. A part of me belonged to Tommy, and it was grey and musty and confused.

After the barley was in, I started hanging round the stop again. I knew that I would find a boyfriend there eventually, and settle down, even though it wasn't what I wanted. Sometimes, when I thought about how I had messed up in The Saints and in the city, I felt my lips purse, a bit like my mum's. I started watching her as she folded and refolded everything in the house that would bend itself in her restless hands. I felt closer to her than I'd ever been. And I wondered what she had or hadn't done when she was young that had left that streak of unspent bitterness in her.

I missed Tommy and his drums. I kept hoping that he'd come back and find me; but then grandad died, and I never heard my proper name again. I hid by the river-bank, but no one ever called me Anne of the ragged lace. So I knew that Tommy wouldn't ever come back for me, because it was my name he'd loved, and not my pallid face.

Lisa St Aubin de Terán
The Bay of Silence £2.95

Rosalind and William have all the appearance of success: a couple of
beautiful people in their thirties, she an actress and he a graphic
designer, revisiting Sestri Levante on the Italian Riviera where they
once spent their honeymoon. But they have been driven there by
paranoia – by a slow dread of what will happen to the two of them
if anyone finds out about their baby Amadeo, whose identity, and
even whose existence, is at the heart of the schizophrenia from
which Rosalind has long suffered . . .

'She has the surrealist's gift for making the mundane exotic'
ISABEL QUIGLY, FINANCIAL TIMES

'I was rather shattered by it . . . it ends up a very macbre and fantastic
book indeed, and I don't think I've really quite got over it yet'
VICTORIA GLENDINNING ON BBC RADIO 4'S KALEIDOSCOOPE

'It draws, inevitably, parallels with *Tender is the Night* and, beside it,
stands up as equal. It is a quiet yet astonishingly powerful and
absorbing novel at the forefront of contemporary British fiction'
BRITISH BOOK NEWS

'Compulsively readable and written with grace and a new authority
which adds to the appeal of this most interesting author'
COSMOPOLITAN

'She combines a powerful sense of place with an unusually
compassionate understanding of human complexity'
DAILY TELEGRAPH

Black Idol £3.99

On a December afternoon in 1929, Harry Crosby, playboy and party-goer, poetaster and patron of the arts, borrowed a friend's apartment to entertain his mistress. How they both came to be found dead of gunshot wounds is an enigma of twentieth-century Americana ... or was until the remarkable Lisa St Aubin de Terán created this extraordinary factional narrative.

From the long dead lips of Josephine Rotch Bigelow we learn of her lover's exotic odyssey – through the horrors of war and the dens of literary lions, a world of black silk stockings and the black idol opium – to that fateful *liebestod* in the Hôtel des Artistes ...

'The atmosphere is thick with the fumes of Cutty Stark ... the narcotic stuff of fantasy' THE OBSERVER

'Continuously absorbing ... an accomplished piece of work' THE FINANCIAL TIMES

'We have world enough, and time enough, for ... novels as original as Lisa St Aubin de Terán's' THE TIMES

Toni Morrison
Beloved £3.99

It is the mid-1800s. At Sweet Home in Kentucky, an era is ending as slavery comes under attack from the abolitionists. The worlds of Halle and Paul D. are to be destroyed in a cataclysm of torment and agony. The world of Sethe, however, is to turn from one of love to one of violence and death – the death of Sethe's baby daughter Beloved, whose name is the single word on the tombstone, who died at her mother's hands, and who will return to claim retribution.

'*Beloved* is Toni Morrison's fifth novel, and another triumph. Indeed, Ms Morrison's versatility and technical and emotional range appear to know no bounds. If there were any doubts about her stature as a pre-eminent American novelist, of her own or any other generation, *Beloved* will put them to rest'
MARGARET ATWOOD, NEW YORK TIMES BOOK REVIEW

'I can't imagine American literature without it. Without *Beloved*, our imagination of the nation's self has a hole in it big enough to die from' LOS ANGELES TIMES

'*Beloved* possesses the heightened power and resonance of myth . . . a dazzling novel' NEW YORK TIMES

'She melds horror and beauty in a story that will disturb the mind for ever' SUNDAY TIMES

'You have to read it.' VICTORIA GLENDINNING, COSMOPOLITAN

'A masterpiece' NEWSWEEK

'This is a huge, generous, humane and gripping novel . . . It is a magnificent achievement. This novel gave me nightmares and yet I sat up late, paradoxically smiling to myself with intense pleasure at the exact beauty of the singing prose . . . it is an American masterpiece' A. S. BYATT, THE GUARDIAN

Graham Swift
Learning to Swim and Other Stories £3.99

'Swift acquires strength from the interleavings and interweavings of
his collection. Almost all the stories are versions of the 'family
romance', protective inventions attempting to cope with the tensions
and rifts within families, whether children and parents or, by
extension, husbands and wives. Children, teenagers, doctors and
patients, a refugee Hungarian boy, a Greek restaurant owner – all are
clearly yet subtly presented, in their obsessions and deceptions'
THE OBSERVER

'An admirable collection. Each story has its subtle nuances of
narrative and language which establish a quite distinct character.
A most impressive work of fiction' THE TIMES

'... among the most promising young writers in Britain ... Graham
Swift should be read by everyone with an interest in the art of the
short story' PAUL BAILEY, THE STANDARD

Graham Swift
Waterland £4.99

'At once a history of England, a Fenland documentary, and a
fictional autobiography . . . a beautiful, serious and intelligent novel'
OBSERVER

'Swift spins a tale of empire-building, land reclamation, brewers and
sluice minders, bewhiskered Victorian patriarchs, insane and
visionary relics . . . a startling cast of characters going about their
business as though it were utterly normal and preparing the way,
down the centuries, for a trio of deaths' BOOKS AND BOOKMEN

'Positively Faulknerian in its concentration of murder, incest, guilt
and insanity' TIME OUT

'One of the most important talents to emerge in English fiction'
GLASGOW HERALD

Josef Skvorecky
The Engineer of Human Souls £7.95

'Magnificent! A magnum opus!' MILAN KUNDERA

'*The Engineer of Human Souls* spins its story from the torn entrails
of Central Europe. Yet what emerges is comedy – black, grimacing
and explosively funny, as peculiarly Middle European as the
despairing wit of Prague's own Franz Kafka. Skvorecky has mixed
history with high unseriousness before – notably in *The Bass
Saxophone* ... but his latest work is unquestionably his masterpiece
of that modern speciality, the heartbreaking belly laugh ... So this is
what the novel has been! So this is what the novel can still be!'
TIME MAGAZINE

'The author's longest and most complex novel; it is his best: humane,
always satirical but affectionate, sparkling with lively intelligence and
good will. He is one of the most independent-minded of all exiles.
Skvorecky's Danny is in part himself: an exile from his country who
finds himself a professor in Canada. He is a kind of intellectual
Schweik, although far less ruthless than the good-natured (not
good-hearted) sergeant. It is picaresque in form. If you feel like
affirming rather than denying in spite of everything: if you feel like
laughing ...' MARTIN SEYMOUR-SMITH, FINANCIAL TIMES

'A huge, multifaceted novel that seems to be no less than a
compendium of the writer's experience of two worlds: the tragi-
farcical world of the police state he left and the safe, prosperous,
shallow, world without history in which he presently lives and
teaches. Mr Skvorecky is indeed an honorable writer – large-souled,
passionate in his response to the atrocities and absurdities of the
age, a writer who never loses sight of what is concretely human
beneath the abstractions of history and ideology'
NEW YORK TIMES BOOK REVIEW

'Nothing is considered unmentionable, whether it concerns dishonest
behaviour, impurity of motive, unseemly farce, foul language or
pungent scatological detail. Stalin is said to have called the writer
the "engineer of human souls" and Skvorecky takes the challenge
seriously, interpreting the phrase in his own ironical manner'
SUNDAY TIMES

Winner of the Governor General's 1985 Award for Fiction in Canada

Mario Vargas Llosa
Aunt Julia and the Scriptwriter £4.99

'Mario, 18-year-old law student and radio news-editor, falls
scandalously for his Aunt Julia, the 32-year-old divorced wife of a
cousin, and the progressively lunatic story of this affair is interwoven
with episodes from a series of radio soap-operas written by his friend
Pedro Comacho, a scriptwriter of prodigious output and hysterical
imagination ... Llosa's huge energy and inventiveness are
extravagant and fabulously funny' NEW STATESMAN

'Pulls off that South American rope-trick with unprecedented power
and skill' SUNDAY TIMES

'A high comedy of great warmth and masterly control of form ...
tough, tender, funny, tactfully erotic, with moments of bitterness,
despair and farce' THE TIMES

'Will confirm the opinion of all those who think that the Latin
American novel is the most vigorous contemporary form at present'
LITERARY REVIEW

Bruce Chatwin
On the Black Hill £4.99

'Nothing in Mr Chatwin's previous work quite prepares us for the
dramatic intensity with which scene after scene of the novel is
brought to light. He belongs, like Lawrence and Hardy before him, to
that line of novelists, poets, diarists and amateur naturalists who
have made the rural life of Great Britain more intimately known to
generations of readers than that of any other country in Europe or
America. The contours of the hills, the outcropping of stone, the
fields and woods, the barnyards, the sudden shifts in the weather,
the passage of clouds and the play of light — all are rendered by
Mr Chatwin with that loving precision and sensuous delight in the
look and feel and names of things that characterize the best writers
in the tradition' NEW YORK TIMES BOOK REVIEW

'It is the first novel I have seen in two years which begins to merit
the accolade of "masterpiece" AUBERON WAUGH, DAILY MAIL

All Pan books are available at your local bookshop or newsagent, or can be ordered direct from the publisher. Indicate the number of copies required and fill in the form below.

Send to: **CS Department, Pan Books Ltd., P.O. Box 40, Basingstoke, Hants. RG21 2YT.**

or phone: 0256 469551 (Ansaphone), quoting title, author and Credit Card number.

Please enclose a remittance* to the value of the cover price plus: 60p for the first book plus 30p per copy for each additional book ordered to a maximum charge of £2.40 to cover postage and packing.

*Payment may be made in sterling by UK personal cheque, postal order, sterling draft or international money order, made payable to Pan Books Ltd.

Alternatively by Barclaycard/Access:

Card No.

Signature:

Applicable only in the UK and Republic of Ireland.

While every effort is made to keep prices low, it is sometimes necessary to increase prices at short notice. Pan Books reserve the right to show on covers and charge new retail prices which may differ from those advertised in the text or elsewhere.

NAME AND ADDRESS IN BLOCK LETTERS PLEASE:

....

Name ——————————————————————————

Address ——————————————————————————

————————————————————————————————

————————————————————————————————

————————————————————————————————

3/87